ROPING IN
THE COWGIRL

BY
JUDY DUARTE

MILLS &
BOON

First Published in Great Britain 2016
By Mills & Boon, an imprint of HarperCollins*Publishers*
1 London Bridge Street, London, SE1 9GF

© 2016 Judy Duarte

ISBN: 978-0-263-92027-7

23-1016

Our policy is to use papers that are natural, renewable and recyclable products and made from wood grown in sustainable forests. The logging and manufacturing processes conform to the legal environmental regulations of the country of origin.

Printed and bound in Spain
by

He could see the wheels turning in her mind, no doubt going over those blasted questions he'd been asking himself ever since that last kiss.

And he sensed the yearning in her eyes, the desire.

"What are we going to do about this?" he asked finally.

"I know what I'd like to do," Shannon said. "But you'll be leaving soon. Right?"

She bit down on her bottom lip, a pensive reaction that sent Blake's blood racing. He suspected she was about to agree to the suggestion he hadn't actually spelled out.

That was, until she looked up, caught his eye and said, "Believe it or not, I'm an old-fashioned girl."

Which meant what? That before making love she wanted a ring, a white lace gown, a walk down the aisle to the altar and a vow that would last forever?

He supposed he couldn't blame her for that. But that wasn't something he could offer her.

They sat quietly for a while, but her words still hung in the air. And so did his desire for her.

He reached for her hand. "I'm afraid that, under the circumstances, I can't give you any kind of commitment. But I can give you tonight."

* * *

Rocking Chair Rodeo:
Cowboys—and true love—never go out of style!

Since 2002, *USA TODAY* bestselling author **Judy Duarte** has written over forty books for Mills & Boon Cherish, earned two RITA® Award nominations, won two MAGGIE® Awards and received a National Reader's Choice Award. When she's not cooped up in her writing cave, she enjoys traveling with her husband and spending quality time with her grandchildren. You can learn more about Judy and her books at her website, www.judyduarte.com, or at Facebook.com/judyduartenovelist.

To J. Frank Astleford, Emily Itzaina,
George Johnston and Emelie Kuehn,
who taught me to love and value the
older generation and all they had to offer.

Your stories about your own grandparents and the
"good old days" made history come alive for me.
You will live in my heart and my memories forever.

Chapter One

He'd been...*fired*? Seriously?

Blake Darnell bent forward in his tufted-leather desk chair and studied the legal document he'd just received in the afternoon mail. He was so caught up in reading what his great-uncle's new attorney had drafted and filed with the Texas court that he only now heard someone speaking to him.

"Did you hear me?" the law firm's administrative assistant asked, her voice rising a decibel.

He glanced at his open office door, where the efficient older woman stood. "I'm sorry, Carol. What did you say?"

She crossed her arms, her expression of curiosity morphing into one of concern. "I asked if there was anything else you needed me to do before I leave, but you were a hundred miles away. Is something wrong?"

Apparently she'd been standing there for a while, long enough to notice the furrow in his brow, the frown on his face. But he shrugged off her question and his penchant for honesty. "No, everything's fine."

"It doesn't look that way to me."

That's because things were actually a mess. What had Uncle Sam been thinking when he'd made this decision? Yet as stunned as Blake was, as angry at the circumstances, a niggle of guilt wormed its way into the mix. And having to assume at least part of the blame didn't sit well with him, especially since he could justify everything he'd done. But it was what he'd failed to do that was most unsettling.

Carol entered his office and made her way to the edge of his desk, the familiar scent of her favorite perfume still faintly clinging to her at the end of the workday. "When I sorted the mail, I noticed the return address on that envelope was from a law firm in Brighton Valley. Does it have anything to do with your uncle?"

Normally, Blake kept his personal affairs to himself, but Carol was an exceptional employee and loyal to a fault. She'd also taken him under her wing six years ago, when he'd first started out at the Beverly Hills law firm of Greenburg, Rawlings and—now that Blake had made partner—*Darnell*.

Before he knew it, Carol had become a second mother to him, baking him homemade cookies and even inviting him to her house for dinner on the weekends. In fact, in many ways, she was more maternal than the one who'd given birth to him.

She'd mentioned retiring a couple of times, which

was understandable since she was approaching her sixtieth birthday. But if and when she actually decided to turn in her resignation, he and the other partners would have a hell of a time replacing her.

Blake blew out a ragged sigh and leaned back in his chair, the springs and leather creaking with his movement. "Apparently Uncle Sam wasn't satisfied with my legal advice or my ability to look over his financial affairs, so he hired another lawyer and has taken back full control of the Darnell Family Trust."

"Is he competent enough to do that?" Carol asked.

"His mental abilities were never in question." Still, Blake suspected the elderly rancher had lost the grip he'd once had on his common sense.

Damn. Was this really happening? Blake pushed back his chair and got to his feet. Then he walked to the window and gazed down at the cars driving along Wilshire Boulevard.

"I'm sorry," Carol said. "I only asked that question because, the last I heard, he'd moved into a skilled nursing facility."

"That was nearly a year ago. But a lot has changed since then. He moved to a retirement home for old cowboys called the Rocking Chair Ranch." And if Blake hadn't been so tied up with those last two cases and had let one of the other attorneys handle them, if he'd gone to Texas and visited his uncle in person, then maybe Sam wouldn't be in this fix.

"A home for retired cowboys should be a fitting place for a man who'd been a rancher all of his life," Carol said.

Blake turned away from the window and raked his

hand through his hair. "Yes, it is. But the Rocking C is also a working ranch. And several months back, my uncle got a wacky job offer to be the foreman."

"That's a surprise—and a nice one." Carol smiled and lifted a single brow, apparently awaiting Blake's agreement.

Instead, he slowly shook his head. "Yeah. But he's pushing eighty."

"As a woman facing retirement age, I'm not looking forward to giving up my independence. After a few weeks of leisure, I'd probably jump all over a job offer that would allow me back into the workforce and let me use the skills I've acquired over the years."

Blake didn't doubt that. From the purple streak in Carol's trendy hairstyle to the multiple piercings along her ears, she did her best to remain youthful and stylish. And while he valued her opinion, this situation was so...personal. The mishmash of feelings he was dealing with kept popping up in his chest, making him feel as though he was playing an unending game of whack-a-mole.

Carol crossed her arms and shifted her weight to one hip. "You were so worried about losing him last year, I'd think that you'd be happy that he's found a new purpose in life."

"Under normal circumstances, I *would* be. But... Well, it's complicated." Blake wasn't sure how much he wanted to share, especially since his feelings were involved.

Okay, so it was his guilt that ate at him the most, and he wasn't sure how to make things right. But Carol knew how much he loved his uncle, how he'd tried his best to take care of him—albeit from a distance.

Two years ago, when Uncle Sam and Aunt Nellie decided to sell their ranch and retire, Blake had tried to talk them into moving to California so he could look after them. He'd even asked Carol to check out various nearby senior communities—all expensive, top-notch places where they'd be safe and well-cared-for. But Sam, who could be as stubborn as that ornery old mule he used to own back when Blake was a kid, had refused to even consider it.

Instead, he and Nellie had remained in Texas, moving into an assisted living complex in Brighton Valley. At that point, they'd signed over their trusteeship to Blake, their only heir. And he began looking over their financial affairs, which were considerable, although most folks wouldn't know it. Sam Darnell might look like a plain and simple cowpoke, but back in the day, he'd been a sharp cattleman, landowner and investor.

After Aunt Nellie suffered a stroke and died, Blake was heartbroken. But what had really torn him up was seeing how badly his uncle took the loss. The couple didn't have any children, so it was just the two of them. And when Nellie passed, Sam lost his will to live.

In fact, his health had suffered so badly that he needed skilled nursing and had to move into a separate medical facility down the road. His doctor told Blake they'd have to call in hospice if Sam continued to lose weight and strength.

Again, Blake had suggested that his uncle move to California, but the stubborn old cowboy dug in his boot heels, insisting he was a Texan—born and bred. And that's where he intended to die.

In what seemed to be a miracle at the time, a nurse's aide managed to connect with him and encouraged him to start eating again. When she inherited a ranch called the Rocking C, she told Sam all about her plan to open a retirement home and asked him to come to work for her as her foreman. But there was more to the story. Things that didn't sit well with Blake.

Carol crossed the room and closed the door to his office, drawing him from his musing.

"Talk to me," she said. "Tell me what's going on."

Blake let out a sigh. "Sam struck up a romance. According to him, she's not only a 'younger woman,' but a 'sexy brunette with sparkling green eyes'. And I'm afraid he plans to give away the farm—so to speak."

At that, Carol scrunched her brow. "A woman he met at the ranch?"

"Her name is Joy, and apparently, she works there, too. As long as I had control over the finances, I would have been able to put the kibosh on any wildass plan he had to whip out his credit card or write a check. But now I don't have a say, so Sam's free to make any crazy financial decisions he wants."

Carol cocked her head. "Isn't it his money to do with as he chooses?"

"Yes, absolutely. And even though I'm supposed to inherit his estate—unless he's changed that, too—I don't care about the money. I already have more than I need. It's the principle of the thing. I don't want to see anyone take advantage of him."

"Do you really think he's that lonely—or that gullible?"

"I wouldn't have believed it before. But he emailed last month and said he wanted to get the woman's teeth fixed. He even mentioned buying her a house. And, apparently, she has a niece who wants to go to medical school, but can't afford it."

"What'd you tell him?"

"I said, 'Absolutely not.' He was talking about spending a lot of money on a woman he'd just met. I can only imagine how she's playing him." Blake had known plenty of gold diggers like that. Hell, he'd almost married one until he'd finally seen through her manipulations.

"Okay, you said you've been emailing him. And I realize you're reluctant to go on vacation, in spite of my advice to take some well-deserved time off so you can fill the well. But have you tried talking to him in person, at least, on Skype or the telephone?"

Blake blew out a sigh. "Yes, I tried calling the ranch a few minutes ago. The woman who answered said he wasn't available, but I heard his voice in the background." Blake turned to Carol, unable to mask his feelings. "Can you believe it? For the first time in my life, my uncle refused to talk to me!"

"Ouch."

"And to make matters worse, I just got sucker punched with this." Blake tapped his finger on the document lying on his desktop. "I'm not sure whose idea this was, but I'm not going to stand by and watch my uncle get taken advantage of by a woman intent upon taking him to the cleaners. I'm going to fly to Texas and check things out for myself."

"Under the circumstances," Carol said, "that's probably a good idea. I'll make your travel arrangements. I assume you'd like to go as soon as possible."

Blake would leave right now, if he could. But he'd have to brief whichever attorney would be covering for him while he was gone.

"What's on my calendar?" he asked.

The ever-efficient Carol smiled. "Nothing that can't be postponed, canceled or handled by someone else, so consider it cleared. You're free for as long as you need to be."

Blake must have appeared skeptical—and hesitant—because she added, "Oh, come on. You haven't taken any significant time off in years. And while this isn't the same thing as a real vacation, at least it will get you out of the office for a while. Some evenings I was afraid we'd have to move a bed into the supply closet for you."

He smiled at the thought—and at the woman who knew him better than anyone probably ever had. "You're one in a million, Carol."

"So are you. And one day, when you finally put that broken engagement behind you, some sweet, unselfish woman is going to see that, too."

"Yeah, well, I'm not interested in striking up another romance—or in finding a sweet, unselfish woman. Right now I'm going to confront that gold-digging, green-eyed brunette who's gotten her hooks into my poor old uncle. So book me a first-class seat on the next available flight to Houston—nonstop."

"Will do," she said. "I hope you plan to stay for more than a day or two."

He'd probably have to. It might take a while to talk some sense into the stubborn yet naïve old cowboy. "Let's make it a one-way ticket for now."

Blake wasn't sure what kind of resistance he was going to meet from his uncle or the woman who'd turned his head, but come hell or high water, when he returned to California, he was bringing Sam home with him.

Shannon Cramer gripped the steering wheel, slammed on her brakes and skidded to a stop as a flat-bed truck spun out in front of her, spilling its precariously stacked load of hay bales onto the road and blocking traffic to the Rio Rico Bridge in both directions. The driver, a befuddled teenager who'd probably just gotten his license, climbed from the cab and gazed at the mess.

Several cars had already lined up behind Shannon, and more than one driver honked. She had half a notion to join in their frustration, but the blaring horns and angry voices weren't going to help or do anyone any good.

Of all days to have this happen. She never over-slept, although for some reason, she'd forgotten to set her alarm last night. And now she was going to be more than just a little late to work.

The wide-eyed teenage boy, his cheeks flushed, pulled the bill of his baseball cap down, as if attempt-ing to hide his face. Apparently he had no idea what to do about the problem he'd caused or the angry motorists he'd inconvenienced, because he slunk back to the cab of his truck and climbed inside. When he placed his cell phone to his ear, Shannon assumed he was calling someone to help him clear the road.

She reached for her own cell to dial the Rocking C and let them know she'd get there as quickly as she could. Only trouble was, the call didn't go through.

That was the problem in this part of the valley. For some reason, the cell tower wasn't able to pick up signals in the low-lying areas. And even if you did manage to get a bar or two, the reception was terrible.

Dang it. She couldn't believe this was happening. She needed to relieve the night nurse at the ranch. Darlene, the LVN, also had a part-time afternoon job waiting tables at the truck stop café along the interstate and needed to get some sleep before she started her shift.

Shannon glanced at her wristwatch, then at all the hay that blocked both sides of the road and the entry of the narrow, two-lane bridge. On any other day, she might have gotten out of her car and started clearing the mess herself. Heck, she'd grown up on a ranch and had been handling hay since she was a kid. But last Friday, while helping an elderly man get out of a rocking chair on the front porch, she'd pulled something in her back. The pain had finally eased and she was feeling much better now, but she didn't dare try to drag eighty- to ninety-pound bales of hay out of the street and risk hurting herself again.

She frowned at the blocked road. Maybe she could encourage a few of the other drivers to help out. She'd no more than opened the door of her Toyota Celica when a couple of lanky cowboys jumped out of their pickup and started toward the chaos. One, who looked remarkably like the champion bull rider who'd been raised on a ranch on the outskirts of Brighton Valley, got right to work.

The other knocked on the window of the teenage driver's door. When the boy glanced up, the cowboy hollered, "Dammit, kid. You passed us two miles back, driving like a bat out of hell. Didn't anyone tell you to tie down a load? Get your butt out here and help us get this cleaned up."

Thank goodness. Still holding her smartphone, Shannon got out of her car, made her way around the hay bales and walked to the bridge, hoping to get a few bars and to have better reception there. After a couple of tries, she finally reached Sam Darnell, the Rocking C foreman. At least, it sounded like Sam's voice through the crackling on the line.

"I'm afraid there's been an accident on the county road," she said. "No one was hurt, but I'm going to be late to work." When Sam didn't respond and the crackling stopped, she lowered her phone and glanced at the display. No Service.

She let out a ragged sigh. The single bar she'd seen moments earlier had completely disappeared. Hopefully Sam got the message and would pass it on.

A few minutes later, as one of the cowboys began to wave the cars through, Shannon slid behind the wheel and started her engine. Finally, she was on her way. Yet while the ranch was only two miles away, she was still twenty minutes late when she pulled into the yard.

As she parked near the barn—which Sam and a couple of hands had painted red last week—she glanced at the clouds that loomed on the northern ho-

rizon. They weren't dark yet, which was good. Whenever heavy rain hit the valley, the bridge washed out,
making it impossible for vehicles to get in or out of
the ranch for days at a time.

The TV weatherman had said the first incoming
storm had stalled and probably wouldn't hit until tomorrow or the next day. But predictions were sometimes wrong. Either way, she had a well-stocked
medical supply room and could handle more than
basic first aid. However, a serious accident or illness
would require a trip to the Brighton Valley Medical
Center, which was forty-five minutes away.

She'd no more than started toward the back entrance of the sprawling ranch house when a late-
model white Lexus pulled up beside her and parked.

That was odd. The ranch owners were out of town
for the next few weeks. And the elderly residents, as
well as the ranch hands who worked at the Rocking
C, didn't get many visitors, especially arriving in
fancy vehicles.

By the time the driver, a handsome man in his
early- to midthirties, got out of the car, her curiosity
had grown to the point that even though she needed
to get inside, she couldn't seem to move her feet.

He wore an expensive suit and fancy loafers—
Italian leather, no doubt. At well over six feet tall,
with blue eyes and dark hair that must have cost him
a pretty penny to have cut at an expensive salon, he
was more than attractive. In fact, he'd be drop-dead
gorgeous if he'd soften his expression with a smile.

Who was he? And what business did he have at
the ranch? There was only one way to find out.

"Can I help you?" she asked.

"That depends. Who are you?"

Shannon, who'd had her fill of frustration for the day, bristled at his rude response and crossed her arms. "Why don't *you* go first?"

His lips curled ever so slightly into a smile, and his expression mellowed a bit, as if he might actually respect her spunk. "I'm Blake Darnell, Sam's nephew."

The California attorney? Shannon had heard about him. He rarely visited Sam and had left the poor man to nearly waste away in the nursing facility in town.

Darnell arched a dark brow. "And *you're…*?"

She let the question dangle a moment before introducing herself. "I'm Shannon Cramer."

His gaze swept over her, traveling from head to toe and back again. He seemed to be assessing her and the pink scrubs she wore.

"A nurse's aide?" he asked.

"An *RN,*" she corrected.

Darnell nodded, then walked to the back of the Lexus, opened the trunk and pulled out a suitcase.

What in the world was he doing with *that*? Surely he didn't plan to stay here. Maybe he came to bring some of Sam's belongings to him.

Before Shannon could question him, Aunt Joy stepped out onto the porch and met Shannon the way she usually did—with a cup of coffee. "Here you go. Fixed just the way you like it—with a splash of cream and a dash of sugar."

"Thanks." Shannon took the mug in both hands, letting the heat warm her fingers from the crisp autumn chill.

"There's pumpkin bread to go with that," Joy said, her voice light, her smile refreshing.

It was nice to see her aunt happy again. Her second husband had left her in dire financial straits after wiping out the nest egg she'd once had. When most people were thinking of retiring, Joy had had to find a job. But since she'd been out of the workforce for more than forty years, she had no way of supporting herself. Fortunately, the Rocking C had needed a housekeeper/cook, and Shannon had told the owners that Joy was the perfect candidate.

And that was true, since Joy's most notable qualifications were her culinary skills and an innate ability to make a house a home. So it had worked out beautifully for everyone involved.

Then Joy met Sam Darnell, who soon put a sparkle in her eyes and a spring in her steps. There was a happy glimmer in Sam's eyes, too. It was heartwarming to see.

"I'm glad you're finally here," Joy told Shannon. "Darlene's eager to go home."

"I know." Shannon took a sip of coffee. "It couldn't be helped. There was a little incident on the road near the bridge."

Joy turned to Darnell and offered him a warm smile, which he didn't return. Instead, he seemed to assess her, but in a far more critical manner than he'd studied Shannon just moments earlier.

Why was that? Joy was one of the sweetest women on the planet, which was one reason her jerk of an ex had been able to take advantage of her.

But then again, Shannon knew that Sam's nephew had called him yesterday, and the foreman had refused to talk to him.

The California attorney cleared his throat. "I don't suppose either of you can tell me where I can find Sam."

"He went out to check a leaky pump in the south pasture," Joy said, her voice soft and kind. "But he should be back shortly."

At nearly eighty years old, Sam Darnell could well afford to retire and take life easy, but he thrived on being useful. And he certainly was. The Rocking C had been a struggling cattle ranch when Chloe Martinez had inherited it. There were back taxes and a second mortgage to pay. But Sam, with his wealth of knowledge and experience, had begun to turn things around in a few short months. They certainly weren't out of the woods yet, but the sweet old foreman had told them not to worry, that everything would be okay in time.

For that reason, Sam reminded Shannon of her father, a good and loving man she'd lost way too soon.

"If you don't mind," Darnell said, as he strode toward the front porch toting his fancy suitcase, "I'll sit here and wait for him."

Actually, Shannon did mind. A *lot*. But she bit her tongue out of courtesy to Sam. She adored the former rancher, who'd become a friend. And if he married her aunt, he'd become a part of the family.

In fact, if Sam and Joy actually did decide to tie the knot, Shannon might have to "accidentally" misplace Blake's invitation.

Because while she couldn't think of anything she'd like more than to help Joy plan the perfect wedding. Sam's nephew was a stuffy, conceited tool, and she wasn't looking forward to adding *him* as a relative!

Chapter Two

The two women continued to stand in the yard, gaping at Blake as though he'd just dropkicked a puppy. But then again, who knew what his uncle might have told them about him?

At first, when the older woman wearing a yellow apron walked out of the house carrying a mug of steaming coffee, he'd thought she might be the one who'd been sweet-talking Sam. She wore glasses and wasn't that close to him, so he couldn't see her eye color. But she was a brunette, which he suspected was due to a recent visit to a local beauty salon. She was also in her mid- to late-sixties, so she was definitely what Sam would call "younger." Still, while she was pleasant enough to look at, Blake wouldn't consider her "sexy."

On the other hand, the nurse had big green eyes the color of new spring grass. Her glossy dark hair was a tumble of curls that flowed over her shoulders and down her back. Even while wearing an unflattering pair of pink hospital scrubs she could stoke a dying ember in a man's soul.

But surely she wasn't the one his uncle had been talking about. Besides, it was also a sure bet that she couldn't have a niece old enough to attend medical school. Still, she was a young brunette and definitely sexy...

Blake shook off that arousing but unwelcome thought as quickly as it struck.

Besides, she'd slapped her hands on her hips and was drilling into him with a critical gaze. It was clear to him that she wasn't sharing the love.

Maybe he'd better take a new tack, sidestepping her and starting at the top. So he asked, "Who's in charge here?"

Shannon stood as tall as her petite stature would allow and lifted her chin. "That would be *me*. I'm the head nurse."

Seriously? She might look ready for battle, but she was just a bit of a thing—not much taller than five feet. She was also in her early- to midtwenties, and the way he saw it, she was too young to be running a retirement home, even if his uncle was in charge of the ranch.

In spite of her obvious annoyance, she had pretty features—a heart-shaped face, expressive eyes, thick dark lashes and a scatter of freckles across her nose.

She wasn't wearing any makeup to highlight her

physical attributes, but she really didn't need to. Her beauty was natural and wholesome.

If he had to guess, he'd suspect that she had a nice shape, although those baggy pants and that boxy top hid it well.

Of course, none of that mattered. Blake wasn't about to be sidetracked from the task he'd set out to do. And since he wanted to get to the bottom of the mess his uncle had gotten caught up in, he couldn't afford to aggravate anyone who might be able to help him, particularly the two ladies standing before him.

"If you'll excuse me," the older woman said to Shannon, "I'll let Darlene know you're here and that she's free to leave."

Then she turned away and entered the house, leaving Blake and the nurse alone.

He had to admit that he hadn't put his best foot forward when he first arrived, but there was a reason for that. He hadn't slept a wink on the flight to Texas. He'd also had a long drive from the Houston airport, which had given him plenty of time to stew over what might be going on here at the Rocking C.

"Are you the ranch owner?" he asked Shannon.

"No, that's Chloe Martinez. She's out of town until mid-December, but she left me in charge."

Blake gave the nurse another once-over. She didn't seem to be the kind of woman who would target an eighty-year-old man for financial gain. But was she capable of detecting an emotional exploitation going on under her nose—and then putting a stop to it?

Her eyes narrowed, and she frowned. Apparently he'd really set her off, although he hadn't meant to.

"I'm sorry if I offended you," he said. "It might seem bright and early in the morning to you, but it's been a long day and night for me, one that began more than twenty-four hours ago."

"A successful investment attorney like you must be incredibly busy." She removed her hands from her hips and folded them across her chest. "I'm surprised you were able to fit in a trip to Texas."

She was right. He hadn't created a successful career and comfortable life in Beverly Hills by taking vacations. And he didn't have any time to waste in the Texas countryside now, even if the sights and sounds of the Rocking C stirred up old memories, reminding him of the ranch he used to visit every summer while growing up.

"In spite of what you've heard or might think," he said, "I've really missed my uncle. And it's high time I came to visit. We have a lot of catching up to do."

"Did Sam know you were coming?" she asked.

"I wanted to surprise him."

She nodded at the suitcase near his feet. "It looks as though you didn't come for a short visit."

"I might stay a while. It depends on how things go."

She again eyed him carefully, assessing his stance and demeanor the way an opposing litigator would do. And for one fleeting moment it seemed as if she'd seen right into his heart.

Okay, so maybe she was astute—and not just a pretty face.

"You know," she said, "rumor has it that you're too caught up in making a buck and living the high

life in the city to ever come to Texas. So I have a feeling your uncle will be surprised to see you."

"He probably will be." Obviously his uncle had
been talking to his coworkers. And he hadn't painted
Blake in a very good light.

Shannon uncrossed her arms and softened her
stance, although the skeptical expression she wore
didn't waver.

This wasn't going well, especially since she was
the one who was "in charge." He'd clearly gotten off
on the wrong foot.

Unfortunately, he'd been loaded for bear when he
came to the Rocking C, which hadn't been the right
approach. So he'd have to do something to change
that—and quickly.

He forced a smile and lightened his tone. "There's
something to be said about family issues and misun-
derstandings. There's a lot more behind them than
meets the eye. And there are usually two sides to
the story."

She arched a brow, challenging him to explain
what his side or his explanation might be. But he
didn't want to get into the myriad emotions that had
been brewing inside him since Sam refused to take
his call yesterday.

It had not only stunned him when it happened, but
just like an unexpected paper cut, it had also sliced
him to the quick. That's why he was determined to
patch things up between them.

When he offered her a slight shrug, rather than an
explanation that would require him to discuss hurt

feelings, she said, "Then let's hope your visit here goes well. Or your vacation or whatever it is."

"For the record, I brought my iPhone and laptop, so I can work from here, if I need to."

At that she smiled ever so slightly. "Good luck with that. The internet access here is sketchy at best, and the cell phone service is even worse."

Then hopefully he wouldn't have to stick around very long, just long enough to put a stop to the greedy schemer's attempt to sway Sam into signing over the proverbial farm, not to mention paying her niece's medical school tuition.

"I'll manage without the telephone and internet," he said, although he wasn't sure how long he could do that and still stay on top of everything he had going on back at the office. Yet even if he couldn't get as much work done as he'd hoped, he'd neglected his uncle for way too long.

The screen door swung open, and a redhead in her thirties walked out onto the extensive front porch without so much as a glance at Blake. "Good morning," she said to Shannon. "Is it okay if I leave now?"

"Yes, I'm sorry I was late."

"No problem." The redhead, who must be the night nurse, blinked her eyes a couple of times and yawned. "I'm going to head home and get some sleep."

"I'll see you this evening," Shannon said.

The redhead had no more than climbed into a small Chevy pickup and started the engine, when Blake's uncle strode into the yard as big as life.

At nearly eighty, Sam Darnell had a thick head

of white hair under his Stetson, a warm glimmer in his blue eyes and a smile that wouldn't quit. But he wasn't smiling now.

He folded his arms across his broad chest and cast an accusatory eye on Blake. "Well, look what the cat dragged in. My new attorney bet me that you'd be here within twenty-four hours of receiving your copy of that document, but I thought he was wrong."

Blake shrugged a single shoulder. He'd taken a red-eye flight out of LA to Houston, so he'd arrived at dawn. Even after the time spent on renting a car and driving to the ranch, he'd still gotten here with hours to spare.

Sam adjusted the brim of his hat. "Looks like I owe my new lawyer twenty bucks, on top of the payment for the work he did."

Blake hadn't expected his uncle to be happy to see him, but he certainly hadn't expected him to be so damn angry. Still, if truth be told, Blake really couldn't blame him. "I owe you an apology, Sam, but just to set the record straight, I don't care about that change in trusteeship. Now that you're as healthy and strong as ever, it makes sense that you'd want to take control again."

Sam's only response was a *humph*.

"We need to talk." Blake glanced at Nurse Shannon before returning his gaze to Sam. He was tempted to suggest they speak in private, but he'd let his uncle make that call.

Fortunately, neither of them had to say anything because the attractive nurse took the hint. "If you'll excuse me, I need to get to work."

Sam, who actually did resemble the robust rancher he'd once been and not the frail old man who'd nearly died last spring, lifted the flat of his hand like a traffic cop. "Hold up, Shannon. Will you check on one of my men before you go inside?"

"Of course. What's wrong?"

Sam blew out a sigh. "Nate Gallagher was helping me dig out the mud from around that old pump so we could repair it, and he had a run-in with a broken beer bottle."

The nurse grimaced, apparently concerned about injury. Then she smiled, transforming her mood completely and putting a glimmer in those pretty eyes. "I hope it wasn't his beer bottle. I heard that a few of the new cowboys you hired can get a little rowdy, especially on their days and nights off."

Sam's grin softened his expression and shaved ten years off his face. "You must have been talking to Rex and Pete. Those old coots usually have something to critique about my new hands."

"Yes, that's where I heard it," Shannon said. "But since two of your new hires ended up in jail last Saturday night and you had to bail them out, I drew my own conclusion."

At that, Sam laughed, again reminding Blake of the man he'd always loved and respected, the man who'd once thought Blake could walk on water—or leap tall LA buildings in a single bound.

"Nate doesn't drink anything stronger than soda pop," Sam said. "Besides, it was a dirty old bottle that had been there for a while, so the cut could easily become infected. I wanted to take him to Urgent

Care to get it cleaned out properly, but he didn't want any part of that."

"Where is he?" Shannon asked.

Sam nodded toward the bright red barn, which appeared to have been recently painted. "When Nate spotted you in the yard and realized I was going to ask you to check him out, he swung around to the back entrance. He's probably washing off the blood and planning to slap a bandage over it. But that cut was pretty deep."

"Then I'll hurry and take a look at it before he covers it up and heads back to work." Shannon lifted the mug she'd been holding, took a sip and then set it on top of an old tree stump near the porch. "I'll be back in a few minutes."

Before Blake could resume talking to his uncle, the screen door swung open and the older brunette returned.

"Can I get you some coffee?" she asked Sam. "You didn't have your second cup this morning."

"Not yet." Sam nodded toward Blake. "I need to speak to Fancy Pants first. Then I'll come into the kitchen and share a cup with you." He winked at the woman. "And if you have any of that carrot cake left over from last night, I'll have a piece of that to go with it."

She laughed. "You got it." Then she went into the house, the screen door shutting behind her.

When the two men were finally alone, Blake said, "Like I said, I owe you an apology."

"Just one?" Sam let out a little snort. "And just what would that be for?"

"Not visiting you more often."

Sam straightened his shoulders, which tugged on his red flannel shirt and made them appear to be just as strong and broad as ever. "Once you went off to law school, you put me and Nellie on the back burner."

Why'd Sam have to mention Nellie? If Blake had felt guilty before, the reminder of his aunt and the fact that he'd been too busy to come to Texas and spend either Thanksgiving or Christmas with the couple during the last five years she'd been alive made it all the worse. And no matter what he said, what excuses he'd given himself, there was no making up for that.

Sam glanced at Blake's suitcase. "You planning to stay here?"

"I thought it might take some time for me to prove to you just how sorry I am. So, yes, I'd like to stay with you, if that's okay. Otherwise, I'll find a place in town."

That seemed to touch the heart of the rugged rancher, at least a little. And for that, Blake was grateful. His aunt and uncle had been good to him while he'd been growing up and had felt neglected by his unfailing focus on his career.

He could argue that he'd offered to move them to California, but neither of them would have been happy leaving Texas. He knew that now, even if the truth of it had escaped him before.

"Well, what are you waiting for?" Sam pointed at Blake's luggage. "Get your stuff and come with me. I don't have all day."

Blake grabbed the suitcase and followed his uncle past the barn and down a short path to a small out-building that also appeared to be freshly painted. The exterior walls were clean and white, and the bright red door was the same color as the barn.

"This is my place," Sam said, as he let Blake inside.

Blake scanned the cozy living room with a small stone fireplace on the outside wall and a built-in bookshelf next to it. His uncle had certainly down-sized. Before Sam and Nellie sold their ranch, they'd lived in a sprawling house on more than five hundred acres of prime grazing land.

"I hope I don't inconvenience you," Blake said.

"You won't bother me. For the most part, I've been staying with Joy in the big house."

Blake's gut clenched. What did Sam mean by "staying with" her?

"You're *sleeping* with her?" Blake had meant to mask his surprise, but the tone of his voice let him down.

"So what if I am?" Sam snapped. "I'm an adult."

"Yes, but..." Blake bit back his response, which would only serve to make matters worse.

"Did you think your generation invented sex?" Sam asked. "Or that I'd outgrown the need for it?"

"Neither," Blake said, although he'd assumed that a man his uncle's age... Well, hell. Clearly his as-sumption was wrong, and he was glad to know that. He'd hate to think he'd ever "outgrow" the need or desire for sex.

"And just so you know," Sam added, "I don't need any little blue pills, either."

Blake had no response for that, other than to hope he'd inherited some of the Darnell strength, stamina and hormones.

"Go ahead and make yourself at home," Sam said. "I've got work to do. We'll have to talk more later."

A nap did sound good. Blake hadn't been able to sleep on the plane.

"Lunch is at the big house at eleven-thirty sharp," Sam added. "I'll see you then."

After Sam left, Blake scanned the ten-by-ten-foot living room, with its brown leather sofa, dark oak coffee table and the colorful Navajo rug that adorned the hardwood floor. The place was cozy and clean, although it was a far cry from the high-rise condo in which Blake lived.

But Blake was prepared to stay as long as it took to bury the hatchet. He'd also do whatever he could to protect Uncle Sam's heart and bank account while he was at it.

And if he had to buy off the gold digger and her niece, then so be it. He'd be damned if he was going to just roll over and let nature— or greed—run its course.

If there was one thing Shannon had learned during her first few days on the job at the Rocking C, it was to be prepared for the unexpected. There seemed to always be one minor crisis or another occurring that would keep her busy from morning until night.

And today had been no different. From the traffic jam at the bridge to Blake Darnell's surprise arrival, nothing had been routine. Even dealing with

Nate's injury hadn't been easy. She'd had to override his objections and insist upon cleaning and dressing the wound properly.

After the cowboy had gone back to work, she'd called Doc Nelson, who'd be coming by this evening for the weekly poker game, and asked him to arrive early so he could take a look at it. In the meantime, the doctor had prescribed an antibiotic, as well as a tetanus shot. So she then had to get into the all-terrain vehicle and drive the injections out to the south pasture, bushwhacking the young cowboy, who'd rolled his eyes but let her do her job.

Once that was out of the way, the rest of her morning went as usual. It was just after noon when she prepared the midday medications. As she passed them out, she took time to visit with each of the elderly men, all of whom she'd grown to care about.

The last one on her med list was Rex Mayberry, one of her favorite old cowboys. She often found him outside, seated in one of the rockers on the porch, so that's where she started her search.

She'd barely reached the screen door when she heard him blurt out a curse. Sure enough, she'd found him. She adjusted the small tray she carried with disposable cups of water and medications labeled with residents' names, then went outside.

As she opened the screen door, the hinges squeaked. Rex, who'd been watching the younger cowboys try to gentle a yearling in the corral, turned and watched her approach. The scowl he'd been wearing morphed into a wry grin. "Well, if it ain't my personal Florence Nightingale. I was beginning to think you'd abandoned me."

"My favorite resident? No way would I ever forget you." She'd only been working at the Rocking C for three months, but everyone here had managed to touch her heart, especially Rex, who could be a real hoot when he wasn't complaining. And even then she got a big kick out of him.

She handed Rex his pill in a tiny paper cup and waited until he'd taken it and chased it down with water. Turning to go back into the house, she spotted Blake Darnell approaching and stopped in her tracks.

He'd changed out of the khaki slacks he'd been wearing earlier and into a pair of jeans. He might be trying to fit in around here, but he was much too polished around the edges. Even the denim didn't make him look like a rancher, let alone a cowboy. And in spite of the fact that both he and his uncle were attractive men, considering their respective ages, they didn't seem anything alike, especially in temperament.

So when Blake tossed a smile at her and again apologized for being rude earlier, it took her by surprise—a rather pleasant one at that.

"I didn't get any sleep last night," he added, "and then I got stuck in some backed-up traffic about two miles from here. Someone lost a load of hay, although it was pretty much picked up by the time I drove through. So that's why I was a little snappish with you earlier."

As much as Shannon wanted to stay angry at him, she'd never been one to hold a grudge. And the fact that he'd been delayed by the same teenage driver who'd spilled hay all over the road made her smile. "I was probably a few cars in front of you when you crossed the bridge, so I can relate to your frustration."

"Can we start over?" He reached out his hand for a proper greeting, and she took it.

The warmth and strength of his grip sent an electrifying tingle zapping along every one of her nerve endings, a physical reaction to his touch that she hadn't expected and didn't appreciate.

Blake Darnell was a charmer, and she wasn't about to allow herself to be roped in by him. But she'd have to agree with her initial assessment. He *was* drop-dead gorgeous when he smiled.

He was also the kind of man who was too busy to spend time with his aunt and uncle, something she found bothersome. Family was important, especially when you didn't have many relatives left.

What she wouldn't give to have one more opportunity to talk to her father.

"Dang it," Rex hollered out. "Would you look at that?" He pointed a gnarled finger toward the younger man in the corral with a bay gelding. "Oh, for cripe's sake. That guy Sam hired doesn't know squat about horses. Will you go down there and give him a few pointers?"

"Me?" Darnell asked the sweet but crotchety old cowboy.

Rex shot him a frown. "No, not *you*. I was talking to Shannon. Who the hell are you, anyway?"

"I'm Blake Darnell, Sam's nephew from California."

"Oh." Rex sat back in his chair, eyeing the attorney. "I heard about you."

Actually, there weren't many people living or working on the Rocking C who hadn't. Sam might be a sweetheart most of the time, but he didn't hold back when he blew a fuse.

Shannon couldn't hide a smile. She loved these old cowboys who had no problem telling it like it was.

"So," Rex said, returning his attention to Shannon. "Are you going to go out there and give that boy a lesson on the right way to handle a horse? I'd do it myself, but I left my cane inside."

"I'm afraid that's not in my job description," Shannon said. "But just so you know, Sam told me he's been working closely with those new hires and expects them all to make good cowboys someday."

Rex swore under his breath. "Maybe those youngsters are still learning the ropes, but they're doing it while they're on the Rocking C's time clock. Why, even a pretty little nurse like you knows way more about roping and riding than those fool kids."

That might be true, but Shannon's days of riding herd were behind her. She had a new career now, one she liked a whole lot better.

She glanced at Sam's nephew, saw him watching her intently. A rush of heat washed over her, warming her cheeks and setting a flutter in her stomach.

"Can I talk to you?" he asked.

As his eyes locked on hers, the tingle in her belly grew stronger. If she had any sense, she'd tell him she had work to do. Instead, she said, "Sure."

He nodded toward the barn. "Can you take a walk?"

The question, the requested private conversation, sent her thoughts scrambling.

What did he have to say to her? Maybe he only wanted to sway her opinion of him and to ask her to intercede with Sam.

"Okay," she said. "I just need to stay within hearing distance of the house."

Blake held out an open palm, indicating an "After you."

She set the tray with the now-empty paper cups on the table next to Rex, then started down the steps, with Blake and his woodsy cologne and musky male scent following close behind.

"So what did you want to talk about?" she asked.

"For starters, I'd like to know more about the Rocking C and my uncle's position here."

"All right. I'll give you the short version. Chloe Martinez inherited this ranch with the idea of turning it into a retirement home for cowboys. She used to work at an assisted living facility in town, the same one where Sam lived."

"So she offered him a job?"

"Actually, she didn't know much about ranching, so she would visit with Sam and ask him questions. As you probably know, he's got a wealth of experience. So he gave her advice about things—like when a cattle broker was trying to cheat her. He's been a godsend to her and to the old men at the ranch."

"My uncle was one sharp rancher."

"He still is. As for the Rocking C, it's not just a

retirement home. It's a working ranch, which provides our residents with a familiar living environment. That's something Chloe realized was lacking at the place in town, especially when it came to men like Rex."

"Are all the residents as cantankerous as that guy?" Blake asked.

"Rex is actually pretty lovable, when you get to know him."

"Is that so?"

"Yes, it is." Obviously, Blake had his doubts. But Shannon adored everything about Rex.

"You said you were in charge," Blake said. "Where's Chloe, the owner?"

"She and her husband are taking classes in graduate programs at the University of Texas, and I'm covering for her while she's gone."

Blake's arm brushed her shoulder, setting off those tingles again. "And you like it here?"

"Yes, of course. But I'd prefer to have a position at the hospital in town. This job is only temporary. Once Chloe and Joe return, they'll take over again."

There had been one benefit she'd received by working here. She'd managed to find a place for her aunt to feel needed again.

Who would have guessed that a romance would spark between Joy and Sam? How sweet was that?

Shannon nearly mentioned that to Blake, but decided it wasn't her place to let him know how happy her aunt and his uncle were. Just thinking about the May-December romance made her smile, especially when she remembered Sam's words when she'd asked if he was happy. "You bet I am," he'd said. "Thanks to your aunt, I'm downright Joy-ful these days."

As Shannon and Blake walked along the side of the barn, he continued to quiz her about life on the Rocking C. "Are all the retired cowboys as critical of the new hands as Rex is?"

"No, not usually. But that doesn't mean they don't enjoy sharing their knowledge about cattle and horses every chance they get to corner one of the younger guys."

"And letting them know when they're doing something wrong?"

"That certainly happens."

As they circled the barn, the crisp breeze blew a strand of hair across her eyes. She tucked it behind her ear, wishing she'd had time to weave it into a single braid before leaving her house.

"Still," she said, "even though Rex was complaining, those new men are working out just fine."

"Did my uncle tell you that?" Blake turned to her, his arm brushing hers again. His gaze zeroed in on her, and her steps slowed.

"Yes, he did, and I believe him. I grew up on a small spread myself, and while I'm no expert, I think some of Rex's complaints are over the top."

"I'm surprised that Sam didn't hire more experienced hands," Blake said.

"That's because Chloe couldn't afford to pay the higher salaries those men required, although we're all hopeful things will start looking up soon." In fact, Sam had refused to take a paycheck for himself, probably for that reason. He understood profit-and-loss statements. So did the owners. That's also why Joe Martinez, Chloe's husband, was getting an MBA. He hoped to learn more ways to generate funds, including donations.

But Shannon had probably said too much already to Sam's nephew, the attorney. So she held her tongue. No need to see him get riled up about that. He seemed to have enough bothering him already.

There was another reason she kept quiet. One she didn't like pondering.

Blake had finally ditched his scowl, and Shannon liked seeing him smile. Especially with that gleam in his blue eyes, the change in expression made him just as good-looking as she'd thought it would.

And if what she'd heard about him was true, he was the worst possible man in the entire world for her to find attractive. To make matters even worse, he might soon be considered family. And she would bet her last dollar he wouldn't be the least bit thrilled to hear that news.

Chapter Three

The brunette wearing the yellow apron turned out to be the ranch cook—and she was an excellent one, at that.

After serving Blake and the residents in the dining room, she returned to the kitchen, where Sam was eating with the hired hands. When she'd first asked Blake to sit at the table with the oldsters, he'd gotten the feeling that his uncle might have come up with the seating arrangement in order to avoid him. But then he'd wondered whether Sam might have wanted to separate the working men from the residents for one reason or another.

Either way, Blake now found himself seated across from Nurse Shannon and flanked by Rex and another elderly man, whose name escaped him.

However, Shannon had just gotten up to take a phone call, so her chair was now empty.

"By the way," Rex said to no one in particular, "there's going to be a rodeo at the Wexler Fairgrounds next spring. It'll be in April, I think. Anyway, I have a friend who works with the outfit promoting it, and he said the head honcho is looking for worthwhile local charities to support. I told him all about Rocking Chair Ranch. He liked the idea of sponsoring us and is going to talk to his boss."

"Good for you," another retired cowboy said. "That's one way to make sure we can keep the doors open. I'd hate to have to move back to that place in town."

If Rex suggested that a rodeo sponsor the ranch, then it sounded as if they might be struggling to keep things afloat. Shannon had implied there were financial concerns about hiring more-experienced hands, but he hadn't realized they feared going out of business. He'd only been here a short while, but he could see why these men would prefer to live in a setting like this.

Moments later, when Shannon returned to the table and took her seat, Blake shot a glance at her, then at Rex. But the old cowboy didn't repeat his announcement.

Did Shannon already know what he'd asked of his rodeo buddy?

Rex elbowed Blake. "Don't hoard all those warm biscuits, Fancy Pants. Pass them down, will you?"

Apparently word had spread that Sam had given Blake that nickname. He found the moniker bother-

some, but he'd have to live with a few verbal jabs—
at least while he was here.

So he shook off his annoyance, reached for the
bread basket and passed it to Rex. "Here you go. Do
you want butter, too?"

"Yep. And the honey, if you don't mind. Thanks."

Blake returned his focus to his plate, which the
cook had filled with a working man's portion of tender short ribs, mashed potatoes and glazed carrots.
He picked up his fork and continued to chow down.

Chow down? He hadn't used a phrase like that in
ages. Not since he was a kid hanging out on Sam's
ranch, tagging along after the cowboys and hoping
to be one himself someday.

Back then, the Western way of life had become
so ingrained in his mind that he'd always returned
home to California at summer's end talking like a
true Texan, a habit that usually hadn't worn off until
Christmas.

Ever since his arrival on the Rocking C, ever since
he'd caught the first familiar whiff of alfalfa and
spotted the cattle grazing in the pasture, he'd found
himself thinking in terms of the cowboy vernacular
he'd favored as a boy. He just hoped he wouldn't have
to stay here so long that he returned to Beverly Hills
talking in a slow Texas drawl. Wouldn't his partners
in the firm give him grief about that.

He reached for his sweet tea and took a couple of
chugs. He'd forgotten how thirst-quenching an ice-
cold glass could be—when it was made just right.

Next he took a warm biscuit from the cloth-covered
basket, split it open and smothered it with butter. He

hadn't had a home-cooked meal like this since... Well, not since his last visit with his aunt and uncle. Nellie had been an amazing cook, too. That's one of the many things Blake missed about her.

Sometimes at a restaurant, although it wasn't often, he'd spot chicken fried steak on the menu and order it for old times' sake. But he'd never tasted anything that could compare with the way his aunt used to make it.

He wondered if the Rocking C cook had a special recipe of her own. He hoped so, but hers might not be able to compete, either.

As he continued to eat his fill, he listened to the lunchtime conversation. Whether the retired cowboys were discussing the weather, the cost of cattle or the best stock-car drivers of all time, they were an entertaining lot.

Still, he was more interested in the pretty RN seated across from him. In fact, he was so downright intrigued by her and the thoughts that had kept her quiet for most of the meal that, whenever he suspected he could get away with it, he would steal a glance her way.

Sometime this morning, while he'd been napping at Sam's place, she'd twisted her long curls into a topknot. He would have preferred to see her hair hanging loose, though. But he did note her delicate neck, as well as a dainty pair of silver hooped earrings that indicated she had a great sense of style.

Not that she or her appearance really mattered. He wasn't going to allow himself to be distracted or to let his focus drift away from the task he'd set out to do.

He'd yet to run across the woman who was chasing after his uncle. All he knew was that her name was Joy. Was she the woman who'd made this amazing meal? It was possible, he supposed. After all, there was that old proverb that said the way to a man's heart was through his stomach. Maybe he'd ask the cook what her name was—that is, if she ever had a free minute. The woman buzzed through the dining room every once in a while, checking on the oldsters, then she would hurry back to the kitchen.

Blake cut into a tender piece of meat, speared it with his fork and popped it into his mouth. Damn, it was good.

"Hey, Shannon," Rex said, drawing the nurse from her musing. "Doc's coming to play poker with us again this evening. Are you gonna give us a chance to win back what we lost to you last week?"

Blake nearly choked. Had he heard that right? Was the head nurse gambling with the elderly cowboys under her care?

"I'm looking forward to it," Shannon said.

Blake lifted his napkin and blotted his mouth. That had to be a breach of ethics.

Rex jabbed his elbow against Blake's arm again. "You want to join us, kid? It's a fifty-dollar buy-in."

Under the circumstances, considering Shannon was playing with men on fixed incomes, those were pretty hefty stakes.

"I'd rather watch," Blake said. "What time does the game start?"

"Around half past five. Right after supper." Rex

pushed his plate aside with a trembling hand. "Some of us can't keep the late hours like we used to."

Blake didn't doubt that. The men probably weren't as sharp as they used to be, either. Surely Shannon had that figured out and was using it to her advantage. And if the Rocking C was actually in financial trouble, there could be other underhanded things going on around here.

Damn, he was glad he'd come to Texas to see this mess for himself—and to rescue his uncle before the whole thing blew up in his face.

Again Blake focused his gaze on the head nurse. Why was she working at a retirement home and not at a hospital or clinic? Had she taken this job to prey on the elderly?

He was going to have to keep a close eye on her, although he was tempted to keep an eye on her for other reasons, too. Even dressed in scrubs, she was too pretty for words.

But then Melissa, his former fiancée, had been an attractive woman, too. After uncovering her real motive for wanting to marry him, he'd learned a hard but valuable lesson—to guard his heart and never take a woman at face value again.

Even if her face was as pretty as Shannon Cramer's.

The ranch cook, who Rex and the other men had referred to as "Miz Hopkins," had no more than cleared the dinner plates and serving bowls from the table, when Doc Nelson, a spry older man with a potbelly and a Santa Claus twinkle in his eye, arrived with a deck of cards and a case of poker chips.

Shannon, who was still wearing her scrubs, returned carrying her purse. Blake was glad to know he'd soon catch her in the act of taking advantage of the men who were her patients, yet at the same time, he couldn't help his disappointment. He didn't like the idea of the attractive nurse turning out to be a thief. Or the suspicion that "Doc" might be in on the ruse.

After Rex placed two dimes and a nickel on the table, and the doctor tossed out two quarters, Shannon pulled out a dollar bill from her wallet.

"I'll need change," she said.

Blake scrunched his brow. "I thought it was a fifty-dollar buy-in."

"That's what we call it," the doctor said. "There's something about playing for coins that just doesn't seem right to us."

"And neither does playing Bingo," Rex chimed in. "When Shannon first got here and suggested it, I said, 'Hell, no. I'm not playing that girly game.'"

Doc Nelson chuckled. "So I convinced Shannon to not only let them play poker, but to let them wager something more valuable than matchsticks, even if it was just coins."

"Let me get this straight." Blake crossed his arms as he addressed each of the men and the woman seated at the table. "A chip represents a dollar, but it only costs a penny?"

"That's right," Doc Nelson said. "You'll need fifty cents to play. So are you in or out?"

Under the circumstances, since there was no longer a need for Blake to sit back and witness an infraction, he reached into his front pocket for some change. "Sure, why not?"

As the doctor shuffled the deck, Shannon took the seat next to him and asked, "Did you get a chance to look at Nate's hand, Doc?"

"Yep, I sure did. You were right, it needed a couple of stitches, so I took care of that and then bandaged him up again. But I'd like you to keep an eye on it. Even with that shot of penicillin, I'm concerned about infection. Especially because he's not likely to complain about pain or swelling."

Shannon cast a frown on the men at the table. "That's because he doesn't want these guys to call him a 'snot-nosed kid who can't take a little discomfort.'"

"Oh, pshaw." Rex slowly shook his gray head. "I only said that to toughen him up. The first week he got here, he was moping around like someone stole his candy. Besides, as far as I'm concerned, those youngsters Sam hired are just a few years out of a diaper."

"And they're all pretty soft," a wiry man named Chuck added. "The Good Lord sure don't make cowboys like He used to. That's for sure."

Blake shot a glance at Shannon and watched her smile. But why wouldn't she? These good ol' boys were pretty comical.

Nearly two hours later, they called it a night. And this time Rex was the winner.

"Okay," Shannon said. "I'd better go home and get some sleep. I'll see y'all in the morning."

Blake decided to see her out. After all, he was

going back to Sam's place anyway. Still, even though he was downplaying his reason for that decision, he had to admit there was more to him wanting to go outside with Shannon than just being polite.

The woman might have lost a quarter or more tonight, but she certainly knew how to play poker.

As Shannon reached under the table for her purse, Blake got to his feet. "I'll walk you to your car."

His suggestion must have taken her aback because her lips parted, and she hesitated a moment. Then she smiled and said, "All right. I just need to tell the night nurse I'm leaving."

"I'll wait for you by the front door."

She tilted her head slightly, as if suspicious of his offer—or maybe surprised by his manners. Who knew what she was really thinking?

And there lay the problem. Blake shouldn't have given a damn, but he felt compelled to learn more about her. Not only about what she was thinking, but what made her tick. Something wasn't right on the Rocking Chair Ranch, and he had a feeling the head nurse held the key.

After briefing Darlene about a change in one resident's bedtime medication, Shannon met Blake in the living room.

His offer to walk her to her car had taken her by complete surprise. Maybe he was just being a gentleman, but she had a feeling he had something on his mind. If so, she'd find out soon enough.

He opened the front door for her, and she stepped out onto the wraparound porch, where a row of empty rockers were lined against the wall and flanked by pots of red and pink geraniums. As he joined her, she took a moment to savor the sights and sounds of the evening. The moon was only a sliver tonight, yet the stars twinkled brightly in the sky. In the distance, a horse whinnied.

Not wanting him to think she was dawdling or trying to eke out more time with him, she started toward her car, her pace slow until he caught up with her.

"So where did you learn to play poker?" he asked.

"My dad taught me. I used to watch him and his buddies play on Saturday nights, and sometimes, when they needed a fifth, they'd ask me to join them."

"Your mom let you do that?"

Shannon wasn't sure how much of her past she wanted to share with him. But she adored Sam and couldn't see any reason to be leery of his nephew. "My mom died when I was six."

"I'm sorry."

"Me, too." She gave a little shrug. "Anyway, my dad taught me a lot of things, poker being only one of them."

They continued toward her car, the soles of their shoes crunching along the dirt walkway.

"Your uncle reminds me a lot of my father," she added.

"Oh, yeah? Is your dad a rancher?"

"Actually, our ranch belonged to my mother's family, so she was the expert on that sort of thing. My dad was a long-haul trucker. But when she passed away, he quit his job so he could stay home with me. And he did his best to work our small spread."

"I really don't remember my dad," Blake said. "He died right before I started school."

Sam had told Shannon that Blake had lost his father in a skiing accident, but she hadn't realized how young he'd been when it happened.

"That's too bad," she said.

Now it was Blake's turn to give a slight shrug. "My mom and I moved in with her mother in California. But she kept in touch with Sam and Nellie, who practically raised my dad. And when I got a little older, she let me spend summers in Texas with them."

"Sam's a great guy," she said. "Just like my dad."

"It sounds like you and your dad are close."

They certainly had been. "Together, we made a good team. We both tackled the household chores, and each week, after cutting out coupons and planning the meals, we went grocery shopping. And on Saturdays we worked in the yard."

Since her dad was always working on or refurbishing a vehicle in the garage, he'd taught Shannon how to change the oil on the pickup, not to mention spark plugs, fuel pumps and flat tires.

Some men, like Mike Cavanaugh, a city boy she'd dated in college, found her "unconventional hobbies" to be unsettling—maybe even demeaning. But she was a country girl at heart, one with varied interests and diverse abilities. And she wasn't going to pretend to be someone else. At least, not again.

As they reached her car, the automatic floodlight attached to the barn came on. Blake's steps slowed to a stop, and he tossed her a heart-strumming grin. "So what did you and your dad do for fun?"

"We watched TV—classic old movies, but mostly all kinds of sporting events." She laughed. "And as you saw tonight, we also played cards, usually poker. But I play a wicked hand of gin rummy."

"Sounds like Nurse Shannon was once a tomboy."

She returned his smile. "I guess you could say that."

Yet in truth, she'd also been a girly-girl at heart. She loved to take bubble baths and fuss with her hair. In fact, she still did.

"Did your dad ever remarry?" he asked.

"No, he'd been so deeply in love with my mom that he refused to even date, saying he'd never be able to replace her."

The handsome attorney continued to study her until the floodlights turned off. Then he took a few steps to the left, setting off the motion detector and turning them back on again.

"So what made you decide to become a nurse— and not a professional poker player or rancher?"

"My dad was diagnosed with cancer about four years ago and fought it for as long as he could. I went with him to all of his medical appointments and was his caretaker at the end." She paused, reflecting on the painful memories that cropped up to replace the happy ones.

"I'm sorry."

She blinked back the moisture that still filled her eyes when she thought about him and that gut-wrenching struggle to live. "It was heartbreaking to see him suffer, so it was almost a blessing when he passed."

Still, her father's death had left a hole in her heart, as well as one in her life.

"So that's when you went into nursing?"

"To make a very long story short, yes." She wasn't about to tell him she'd once planned to be a doctor, that she'd actually applied and been accepted to several medical schools. But that dream had faded when her father's courageous and costly battle with cancer had drained their savings and caused them to lose the ranch.

After he died, she hadn't wanted to take on huge student loans and had become a registered nurse instead, which to her way of thinking, was the next best thing.

As Blake stood in the soft amber glow, Shannon studied him carefully, the way he stood tall, his shoulders broad. She felt a strong attraction to him, even though she'd yet to completely trust him as Sam's loving and loyal nephew.

But she couldn't allow herself to be swayed by his handsome features, by that glimmer in his blue eyes. As his gaze locked on hers, her breath caught, and her heart raced to a dizzy beat.

If she remained out here with him any longer, things could shift easily into a romantic direction, at least on her part, so she nodded toward her Toyota Celica. "I'd better go. It's getting late, and my workday will begin before you know it."

Blake reached for the handle and opened the car

door—another gentlemanly move. "Then I'll see you tomorrow."

Yes, he probably would, since it appeared that he'd moved in for an indefinite amount of time.

As she slid behind the wheel and started her engine, a sense of loneliness settled over her. What she wouldn't give to have a special man in her life, someone just like her father, who would do anything for her, even if that meant giving up his job and taking over a ranch that he had no interest or experience in running.

But Shannon's dad had been one in a million, and she feared she'd never find anyone who could compete with his memory.

Yet as she pulled out onto the driveway, she glanced into the rearview mirror, spotting Blake Darnell who continued to stand in the yard, hands resting on his narrow hips as he watched her leave.

For one brief moment, she wondered if he might be a man like his uncle...

No, she hadn't seen any real evidence of that. Still, it would be nice to have someone to go home to each night. She just hoped the Good Lord hadn't thrown away her father's mold—and that she'd find a man like him when she least expected to.

The next morning, Shannon arrived at the ranch, and this time, as usual, she was ten minutes early.

As she shut off her engine, she glanced at the clouds on the horizon. There seemed to be more of them today—and a bit darker than they'd been yesterday. But they certainly didn't appear to be the kind that threatened to rain. At least, not yet. Still, she'd packed an overnight bag and left it in her trunk, just in case the first predicted storm hit and flooded the road so she couldn't leave the ranch.

She'd no more than reached the porch when the front door swung open and Aunt Joy met her. Only this time, she wasn't smiling or holding a mug of coffee.

"What's the matter?" Shannon asked.

"Rex fell in the shower a few minutes ago and really banged himself up."

"Oh, no."

Joy stepped aside, allowing Shannon to enter the house. "He cut his head, and it bled something fierce, but Darlene managed to get it stopped."

Darlene could handle most minor, everyday injuries or illnesses. But Joy was clearly concerned.

"Where is he now?" Shannon asked.

"In his room. Darlene stayed to keep an eye on him until you arrived. He's insisting that he's fine, but we'll feel much better when you check him out."

Shannon would feel better, too. As she walked down the long hallway that led to several of the bedrooms, Joy followed along, filling her in. "We think he hit his head on the toilet, because he split his brow wide open. He didn't pass out, but he might need stitches. Darlene told him that she'd let you make that call."

Shannon might not be a doctor, but her coworkers and the men who lived here looked up to her and trusted her opinion, which served as a reminder that she'd given up her dream of going to med school.

When she reached Rex's open bedroom door, she spotted Darlene standing near the twin-sized bed, where the old man lay stretched out. His color was good, and his chest rose and fell at a steady pace.

He turned his head toward the doorway and clicked his tongue. "Would you tell them to leave me be and go on about their business? I just took a little tumble."

Shannon moved closer and studied the head wound, which was no longer bleeding. It could probably use a couple of stitches, but a butterfly bandage might also do the trick.

"It doesn't look too bad," she said. Then she nodded toward the open doorway, letting Darlene know she wanted her to follow her out and into the hall.

When they'd all walked away from Rex's room, Darlene said, "I suggested we take him to the medical center, but he got so red in the face and pitched such a fit that I thought he was going to have a stroke or a heart attack. So I let it go and waited for you to get here and deal with it. You have a way with him."

That was true. For one thing, Shannon wouldn't have suggested that Rex visit the hospital ER without being sure it was absolutely necessary. The man hated sitting around waiting, and he was a terrible patient. He also hated doctors, which had surprised her since he and Doc Nelson had been poker buddies for years.

"I need to check something on the stove," Joy said. "But before I go, what do you think? Should we call an ambulance just to make sure he doesn't have a concussion?"

"No, I didn't see any indication of that. I'll just watch him closely for a while."

Joy nodded, then left Shannon to discuss her medical decision with Darlene.

"That wound really isn't too deep," she said. "I'll clean it up and bandage it, which should work just fine."

"That's probably the best thing to do. Just getting Rex into a car for the ride into town would probably raise his blood pressure sky-high." Darlene rolled her eyes. "For a man who can be sweet as honey at times, he sure can cuss a blue streak."

Shannon chuckled and nodded in agreement.

"Since you're here to relieve me," Darlene said, "I'm going to leave. I'm off tonight, but the last I heard, Maria, who covers for me, had the stomach flu. If she can't make it, give me a call."

If Maria was sick, Shannon wanted her to stay home until she was completely well. She didn't want to risk any of the residents catching it. "I'll check with Maria. If she can't make it, I'll find someone to cover your shift. Enjoy your time off."

"Thanks," Darlene said, as she headed down the hall.

Shannon followed her as far as the living room, then went to the kitchen for her morning cup of coffee.

There she found Sam, talking to her aunt. When Shannon entered the room, Sam asked, "How's Rex doing?"

"I think he'll be fine. But just to be on the safe side, I think I'd better ask Doc Nelson to come by and check in on him."

Sam blew out a slow whistle. "Rex has always been a stubborn old coot, even when he was younger and not so set in his ways. But I'm afraid you're going to have a big fight on your hands. You know how he feels about doctors and hospitals."

She sighed. "Well, then I'll ask Doc to stop by for a casual visit. We won't let Rex know that he's being examined."

Sam slipped his arm around Joy and gave her a tender squeeze. It warmed Shannon's heart to see the older couple, each of whom had suffered heartbreak in the past, find happiness together.

Just watching the two of them make sweet talk and cuddle in the kitchen made Shannon wonder if someone might come along who would put that kind of light in her eyes, warmth in her chest and smile on her face.

But there was no use in dreaming about anything like that. As the back door creaked open, and footsteps sounded in the service porch, Shannon glanced at the doorway just in time to see Blake saunter in, a dazzling smile on his face. Her heart did a crazy little swan dive, and for a moment, she wondered if maybe he might be the man to light that spark.

That is, until Blake gazed at Sam and Joy. In the blink of an eye, his expression went from sweet and charming to blatantly annoyed.

Apparently, he had a burr under his saddle. And when he looked at Shannon, you'd think he blamed her for putting it there.

Chapter Four

Blake wasn't sure if it was his loyalty to Aunt Nellie or his worry about Sam being duped that threw him off balance when he spotted his uncle in an affectionate embrace with the ranch cook.

Both, he supposed.

He tried to rein in his surprise as well as his irritation, but he wasn't having much luck.

"So Ms. Hopkins's first name is *Joy*," he said. Not that he hadn't considered the possibility, but damn. He hadn't wanted her to be the cook.

His uncle stepped aside, yet his arm remained around her waist, and he continued to hold her close. "Yes, this is Joy Hopkins, my intended."

The woman seemed pleasant enough, but Blake still struggled with the relationship because of all the money his uncle planned to spend on her. Still, he had to admit, she was skilled in the kitchen. Maybe that's what had caught Sam's attention, especially since he had to be missing Nellie's meals.

Sam broke eye contact with Blake and turned to Joy. "Honey, I'd like to formally introduce you to my wayward nephew."

She flashed a smile, revealing straight teeth. "It's nice to officially meet you."

Blake had only caught a quick glance at her pearly whites before, but now that he'd gotten a better glimpse, he realized she must be sporting a new set of expensive veneers. Sam had mentioned wanting to "fix" her teeth. Apparently he'd already done so.

In one of Sam's earlier emails, he'd also mentioned buying her a house. And as if that wasn't enough, he'd said he'd like to send her niece to medical school. What other expenses were in the works?

"Why don't you and I step outside?" Sam suggested.

"Good idea." They needed to talk, and Blake didn't want to do it in front of Joy. Nor did he want Shannon to be privy to their conversation.

And speaking of Shannon, what had she been smiling about? Was she actually okay with *this*? Didn't she see anything wrong with a man Sam's age getting hoodwinked by a greedy younger woman?

As Sam headed for the service porch and out the back door, he snatched his worn Stetson from the hook on the wall. Blake followed him outside and into the morning sunshine, wishing he had a hat to shade his eyes.

Once they were away from the house, Sam turned

on him and scowled. "What in the hell is your problem? Didn't I teach you any manners when you were a kid? A little common courtesy in there wouldn't have cost you a damn thing."

"I'm sorry." Blake raked a hand through his hair and blew out a pent-up sigh. "It's just that this new relationship of yours has happened so fast. It's a lot for me to wrap my brain around."

Sam placed his hat on his head, adjusting it to tilt just right. "In case you didn't realize it, I don't have a lot of time to waste if I want to get married again."

"That's the trouble," Blake said. "Why do you need to get married?"

"Because I love her."

How could he be so sure—and so soon?

"What about Aunt Nellie?" Blake asked.

"She's gone, son. And I was heartsick when she passed. But don't I deserve to be happy again?"

"Yes, you do." But how could Blake make sure Sam wasn't being hoodwinked? "Can you give me some time to get used to this?"

"I suppose so. But you owe Joy an apology. You were rude just now, and I'm sure you made her feel uncomfortable."

"You're right. It's just... Well, seeing you two together like that took me by surprise."

Sam folded his arms across his chest. "I've been spitting mad at you for the past few years—and even more so lately. You seemed to just turn your back on me and Nellie without a second thought, choosing a fancy life in the city. To tell you the truth, I'd hoped you'd take over my ranch for me. But that's okay. I realize you have different interests. It's just that your career became the only priority in your life."

He hadn't meant for that to happen. Nor had he meant to neglect Sam and Nellie.

"I'm sorry," Blake said. "I didn't mean to lose sight of the people I love. I hope we can put this behind us."

"So do I. But that's not going to happen if you don't give Joy a chance. It's the least you can do for me."

That was true. And it was only fair. Trouble was, Blake already suspected the worst about her, so it was going to be difficult. But he'd give it his best shot—for Sam's sake.

"If it helps," Sam added, "I never thought I'd be this happy again. And it feels good. *Damn* good."

That did help. Blake just hoped his uncle's happiness was real—and lasting.

"I truly wish," Sam said, "that one of these days, you'll fall in love and get to feel the same way I do."

Blake must have looked skeptical because Sam added, "Believe it or not, there are plenty of women out there who will love you unconditionally, son. And I should know. I've found two of them myself."

His uncle had certainly found *one*. But as far as Blake was concerned, the jury was still out on the second.

"Don't forget," Sam added, "you're the only one left to carry on the Darnell family name, so you'd better get your focus out of the office and start looking to find a woman who'll make you happy."

"Don't worry about me. I might be a workaholic, but I find time to date." In fact, he'd had several relationships, the most serious of which had been a disaster and had turned him off love and marriage.

To make matters worse, his mother's second marriage wasn't particularly happy. So who could blame him for being leery?

"I hope you're right. Maybe there is a woman who'd make me feel that way." If Blake could find someone like Aunt Nellie, he might consider making a lifetime commitment.

But maybe the kind of love and marriage that Sam and Nellie had found didn't exist anymore—or at least, he'd yet to see anything like it.

Sam slapped a hand on Blake's shoulder and chuckled. "And if that woman also happens to cross your eyes and curl your toes at the same time, then you'll know that it's a forever kind of love."

That was clearly what Sam believed he'd found again. Blake hoped that his uncle would prove to be right. Otherwise, the poor old man was in for heartbreak.

And Blake was afraid that another one just might kill him.

Blake had planned to apologize to Joy after lunch, after everyone else cleared out of the kitchen, giving them a little time alone in there. And while he was at it, he'd intended to ask for Shannon's forgiveness, too. He didn't like the idea of her thinking he was a jerk, even though he'd probably left her with that impression of him.

But twenty minutes after Sam had taken the ATV

out to repair a section of downed fence, he'd returned and asked Blake to do him a favor.

"Sure," Blake had said. "What do you need?"

"I have a long list of supplies that need to be picked up in town, as well as some ranch errands to run. You'll find a detailed list on my desk in the barn. I was going to do it myself, but something's come up and I have to babysit my crew."

"I'd be happy to run into town for you, although something doesn't quite make sense."

"What's that?"

"You never used to hire hands who needed to be watched over so closely."

"Yep. You got that right." Sam lifted the brim of his hat, then adjusted it on his head. "But when I had my own spread, I could afford to hire the best men around."

His uncle had just validated what Shannon had mentioned earlier. "So the Rocking C isn't in the best financial shape."

"Not yet, but we're working on that."

"How?"

"Rex has a few connections with a rodeo outfit, and we think they're going to sponsor us. It's not a done deal, but it's looking good."

At least Sam hadn't planned on bailing out the ranch himself.

Blake reached into his pocket and pulled out his keys.

"Put those away," Sam said. "Don't even think about driving that fancy car of yours. Take the old gray Dodge Ram. The keys are hanging on the hook near my office door."

* * *

Glad to have his uncle's trust and to have an opportunity to do something helpful, Blake had gone in search of the list, only to find that it had been longer and even more detailed than he'd expected. Then he'd driven into Brighton Valley, starting at the hardware store and ending at the post office. By the time he got back to the ranch, it was dark.

When he entered the back door to the house, he found Joy in the kitchen. Dinner was over, and she was alone. And surprisingly, she'd kept a plate of food warm for him.

"Thank you," he said. "But before I wolf that down, I want to apologize for being a jerk this morning."

At that, she brightened. "That's okay."

Actually, it really wasn't. Apologies, even ones he'd been contemplating all day, didn't come easy to him. But he'd thought long and hard about what Sam had said earlier, and his uncle was right.

Blake cleared his throat and pressed on. "I loved my aunt, and seeing my uncle with someone else really threw me for a loop. But I shouldn't have reacted rudely."

"I know how special Nellie was. Sam talks about her a lot. In fact, she sounds like the kind of woman I would have liked to have as a friend. So I can understand your surprise—and uneasiness. I hope you'll give me a chance to prove to you how much I care for your uncle."

How could he object to that? Besides, just as he'd

told Sam, he'd like to put a lot of things behind him. But there was one more apology that needed to be made.

"Is Shannon around?" he asked.

"She's already gone home. And tomorrow is her day off."

A sense of disappointment swept over him. He wished he could say it was because he'd have to postpone the apology he owed the head nurse. But it was more than that.

"I was just going to turn in for the evening, so if you don't mind, I'll let you serve yourself." Joy pointed to the plate she'd left on the stove.

"No problem. I'll clean up and lock the door before I go."

"Thank you." The smile she wore as she turned to go made her appear more than just pleasant.

If character was built solely upon culinary skill, then Joy Hopkins was one fine woman. But Blake wouldn't be taken in as easily as his uncle had been. However, going forward, he would make more of an effort to be polite to her.

Once Sam learned that Blake had set things right with Joy, they would reach a truce. Still, the fact that things were better between them didn't mean Blake was ready to return to California just yet.

After eating breakfast with the cowboys, Blake decided to take a walk. If the ranch was in serious financial trouble, he hoped to get a better sense of it after checking things out for himself.

He'd no more than reached the place where the workers and visitors often parked their vehicles when he noticed Shannon's car flanked by a faded red sedan and a gray pickup with gun racks.

He hadn't seen Shannon at breakfast and was told she wasn't working today. Had she left her vehicle here last night? Or had she returned this morning?

If she was around, he should probably apologize to her for his rudeness yesterday, something he hadn't been able to do yet. In the meantime, he continued his walk and his inspection.

About fifty yards beyond the barn sat an unattached garage, its door raised. If he'd seen a ranch pickup or a John Deere tractor parked inside, it wouldn't have struck him as out of the ordinary.

Instead, he spotted someone working on a classic T-bird. The car itself was enough to command his attention, but what really piqued his interest was the "someone" bent over the engine wearing a pair of tight jeans that hugged her shapely hips.

In spite of his plan to scope out the ranch, he studied the woman for a moment, intrigued by her nicely rounded backside.

As if suddenly sensing his appreciative perusal, she straightened and looked over her shoulder.

Well, what do you know? It was Nurse Shannon, who seemed to be as surprised to see Blake as he was to see her.

A few strands of dark hair had come lose from her ponytail. Yet what really drew his eye was the way her snug black T-shirt molded to her upper body, revealing a curvy, feminine shape. The T-shirt was a heck of a lot more flattering than the baggy scrubs she'd worn the past few days.

Her hands, or rather her fingers, were dirty from the work she'd been doing on the car. She brushed them together, then wiped them on her denim-clad hips and said a casual "Hello."

When Blake had gathered his wits and hog-tied his hormones, he asked, "What are you doing?"

She folded her arms across her chest and cast him a frown. "Don't worry. I'm not being lax on the job. It's my day off."

"I know. I met the other day nurse at breakfast." Apparently, he wasn't the only one who thought he owed her an apology. So he made his way toward her.

"That's a great car," he said, checking out the 1957 classic. "Does it run?"

"Not yet, but it will."

She was full of surprises. Even in work clothes and with a smudge of grease on her face, she was attractive.

"So," he said, trying his darnedest to shake off her mounting appeal, "you not only heal the sick and wounded, you refurbish old cars, too."

She shrugged a single shoulder. "It's sort of a hobby, I guess. When I moved to an apartment in town, I didn't have any place to store it. So Chloe let me keep it here."

"You're a woman of many talents." He meant it as a compliment, but her skeptical expression suggested she wasn't buying it.

"Actually," she said, "this car was my father's project. He died before he could finish it."

"So you're completing it for him." As a tribute and

a memorial, he suspected. It was an easy conclusion to come to, and he couldn't help but admire her for it.

"By the way," he said, "I've been meaning to talk to you. I was rude yesterday. My uncle called me out on it, and I told Joy I was sorry. I owe you an apology, too."

Her expression softened. "You're forgiven. I hope you and your uncle have worked out your differences. You're a nicer guy to be around when you're not cranky."

He smiled. Then without revealing his motive, he continued to close the gap between them. In spite of his interest in the vintage vehicle, the nurse intrigued him more.

"So," he said, "thanks to your father, you're a woman of many talents."

"He taught me a lot when I was growing up." She tucked a loose lock of hair behind her ear, the lobe boasting a pearl stud. "How about you? What are you up to this morning?"

"I was taking a walk. When I noticed the garage door was up, I thought I'd stop and take a look. It's amazing what you've done so far."

At that, she finally smiled. He had to admit that it felt pretty darn good to be on the receiving end of it. He continued to study those expressive green eyes, the splatter of freckles on her nose. Even with a smudge of grease on her face and messy hair, she was more appealing than most women. At that realization, his lips quirked into a grin.

Shannon was the first to break eye contact and

turn away. She lowered the T-Bird's hood, snapping it shut.

"Are you done working on it for today?" he asked.

"I hadn't planned to be, but I bought the wrong spark plugs. So now I'll have to drive to the auto parts store and order some new ones."

"Since that's the case, why don't you join me on my walk?"

She seemed to ponder the unexpected suggestion. Finally she said, "Sure. Why not? Just give me a minute to clean the grease from my hands."

"Wait." He reached out and, using his thumb, swiped at the smudge on her face.

At his touch, her breath caught and her lips parted.

"Sorry," he said. "I couldn't help doing that." He was feeling a little surprised himself.

Her cheeks flushed to a rosy hue, and she fingered the side of her head, behind her ear, where she'd tucked that loose strand of hair just moments before. "I must be a mess."

Actually, Blake thought she looked pretty damned cute. Not that he'd mention it. Why throw out a compliment she might misconstrue, one he couldn't possibly follow up on?

"You look fine," he said. "I'll wait here while you wash your hands."

Shannon had no more than disappeared into the barn's rear entrance when Sam spotted Blake and headed toward him.

"I've been looking for you," his uncle said.

"What's up?"

"A buddy of mine has a problem and needs your

help. His family wants him to move to Arkansas, and they've been pressuring him to leave the Rocking C. He's afraid they'll go behind his back and talk to his doctor."

"Okay, but I'm not sure what I can do to help." Blake understood a family's concern when it came to having an elderly relative who wasn't in the best of health.

"He needs legal advice, and he doesn't have a lot of cash, so he can't afford an attorney on his own. I thought you could talk to him and maybe offer him some peace of mind."

Under the circumstances, Blake found himself siding with the man's family, although he'd be damned if he'd mention that and re-create any issues he'd once had with his uncle.

He probably ought to suggest the man contact one of several agencies that offered free legal advice, but mentioning that alternative also could jeopardize the tenuous truce he and Sam had reached. "I suppose I could talk to him. What's his name?"

"Rex Mayberry. You can usually find him rocking away on the front porch every afternoon and criticizing my new hands. But he took a fall yesterday and has been sticking close to the house."

"I know who Rex is." And if anything, Blake would encourage him to listen to his family and consider a move. But he wouldn't say anything to Sam about that. Not when he planned to try and convince his uncle to return to California with him for the same reason Rex's family wanted him to be closer to them. "I'm not sure how much good it will do. He seems pretty stubborn. But I'll talk to him."

"Thanks. I'd appreciate that. Now I'd better check on my new hands before Rex gets wind of any of their perceived shortcomings and raises hell with me for hiring them again."

The two men shared a smile, then Sam turned and walked away. He'd barely reached the corral, when Shannon came out of the barn. She'd washed her hands and face. She'd also combed her hair and had woven it into a stylish twist.

"Where to?" she asked.

"I didn't have a route or a game plan in mind. Why don't you give me a tour of the ranch?"

She studied him a moment, as though he'd gone daft, then a slow smile slid across her face, sparking a glimmer in her eyes. "All right. Let's start with the vegetable garden."

Blake couldn't see that as a point of interest, but he walked beside her and watched as she pointed out the fenced-in area that protected long rows of various plants, where one of the elderly residents was tying up tomato vines.

Curious about the elderly gardener, Blake asked, "Who's that?"

"His name is Gerald McInerny, but everyone calls him Mac. He enjoys being outdoors and tending the garden. Thanks to his green thumb and Joy's skill in the kitchen, we can count on having lots of healthy and tasty local produce in our meals."

Mac, who wore a red long-sleeved shirt and a pair of dirt-stained overalls, glanced up and waved at Shannon. Then, after stretching out the kinks in his back, he returned to his work.

"Come on," Shannon said, "I want to show you something else."

She led him to the corral, where a young hand worked with a yearling. About twenty feet to the left, several lawn chairs had been set up on a patch of grass. Two elderly men, one wearing a veteran's cap and the other a battered Stetson, sat together, watching the cowboy.

"That's Dennis and Ralph," Shannon said. "If we stay here long enough, you'll hear them shout out instructions and criticisms every now and again."

"Actually, I've already had the pleasure of watching Rex do that same thing a couple of days ago."

Shannon lifted a hand to shield her eyes from the sun, which had moved out from behind a gray cloud. "Normally, Rex would be out here with them—if he hadn't fallen yesterday."

"Sam told me about that. Is he doing okay?"

"He's a little bruised and battered, so he's moving pretty slow. But he's on the mend. Still, I'm keeping an eye on him."

Blake and Shannon continued to walk along a pathway that led away from the house and yard.

"Do you know anything about Rex's family wanting him to move to Arkansas?" Blake asked.

"Yes, but he's determined to stay on the Rocking C. That's why he's always fought me on seeing the doctor."

That was one more reason for the man to move closer to his family. If he refused to seek medical care, he wasn't taking care of himself. "Wouldn't Rex be better off near the people who love him?"

"Maybe. But shouldn't he have a say in where he lives?"

"Not if his health is at risk—or his mental capacity is slipping."

"As far as Rex is concerned, we're taking good care of him here. And while he has some issues with his balance and his health, he's pretty sharp."

"But family is important."

Shannon stopped, her abrupt motion causing Blake to slow his steps. "You don't have to tell me how important it is. I don't have any siblings, and I've lost both of my parents. But even then, I wouldn't insist that my aunt move to Timbuktu when she clearly didn't want to go."

"Arkansas isn't halfway across the world."

"It might as well be—if you ask Rex. Besides, there's a lot more behind the story. His relatives insisted that his brother move so they could take care of him. But they took it too far."

"What do you mean?"

"They kept him on life support much longer than they should have, at least that's what Rex said. And he's afraid they won't let him die with dignity."

"Then I can understand why he'd be worried."

They walked along, their thoughts to themselves.

Moments later, Shannon slowed to a stop and asked, "Have you ever been to other retirement homes or assisted living complexes?"

"Yes and no." He didn't want to admit that Carol, his administrative assistant, had done the visiting.

He'd only looked over the brochures of the places she'd culled out for him. "When my aunt and uncle retired and sold their ranch, I'd wanted them to move to California to be closer to me. That way I could look out for them easier. So I was doing some online research, but they chose to move to that assisted living complex in Brighton Valley instead."

Shannon began walking again. "The Sheltering Arms is a nice place for seniors to live, and it used to be one of the only options local people had when choosing a retirement home. But the men who are now living here were once rodeo cowboys, cattle hands and rugged ranchers. They didn't like living in small apartments in town."

Blake scanned the vast pastures, which were dotted with cattle. The acreage could support a lot more of them, although he suspected the ranch finances wouldn't.

They continued talking as Shannon showed him the pump that Sam and one of the hands had recently fixed—and not replaced. Again, Blake wondered if that meant he could believe what had been implied—that the Rocking C was struggling financially.

"I have to admit," he said, "when I heard my uncle was working at a retirement home for former cowboys, I never expected anything like this."

"I know." Shannon brightened, and her voice betrayed her enthusiasm. "I was amazed when I first saw it, too. Chloe wanted to offer the residents a bit of their past, and also allow them to maintain their dignity. Her idea was born from the friendship she struck up with your uncle when she worked at the Sheltering Arms."

He supposed that had become part of the Rocking C's mission statement. No wonder Sam was so all-fired determined to make sure Rex was able to remain here and not move to Arkansas. "Chloe sounds like a bright, innovative woman."

"She is. You'd like her—if you met her."

Something told him that was true, which brought up a question. "Where did you and Chloe meet?"

"In nursing school. When she and her husband both decided to attend graduate school in Houston, she didn't want to leave the place in just anyone's hands, so she asked me to step in."

If that was the case, the owners must have felt that Shannon could handle anything that came her way. And Blake was beginning to think that might be true.

"But as soon as Chloe and Joe return home for good," Shannon said, "I'll be on my way."

"You don't want to continue working here? You have a way with these guys, and they seem to really like you."

"Thanks. To be honest, I've considered staying on, but I really think working in a hospital setting would be the best place for me. Still, I like it here. If I were a retired cowboy or rancher, I'd much rather live here than in a rest home."

Blake could see why the men liked it here. He could also see why it would appeal to his uncle. In fact, he might like to live out his last years on the Rocking Chair Ranch, especially if he could eat meals prepared by Joy.

A slight breeze kicked up, ruffling Shannon's hair and stirring up the scent of her shampoo, something soft and floral that made him envision walking barefoot with her in a colorful field of wildflowers.

He stole a glance her way, watched her brush a loose strand from her eyes. There was another reason a man, no matter his age, might want to stay on the Rocking C. The head nurse was a real beauty, especially in an outdoor setting.

For a moment he found himself pondering the wisdom of hanging around a while longer. It was tempting, especially if he could be on the receiving end of Shannon's tender loving care.

Chapter Five

By the time Shannon had shown Blake around the Rocking C and they returned from their walk, big gray clouds had begun to move into the valley, stealing the sunshine that had warmed the morning chill just an hour earlier. Shannon was willing to bet that it would be raining by nightfall.

As she and Blake reached the yard, she spotted Nate Gallagher, the man who'd cut his hand while helping Sam repair the old pump. He'd just unsaddled his gelding and was turning the horse loose into the corral nearest the barn.

"Hey, Nate!" she called out. "How's your hand?"

The dark-haired cowboy glanced up. "It's coming along just fine. Doc insisted on stitching it."

"Are you supposed to be working yet?" she asked.

He lifted a leather-gloved hand. "I've got it taped up and protected."

"Good. It's going to heal better that way." She didn't mention that she'd been the one to push for Doc's examination of his wound and offered him a smile instead. "If you don't mind, I'd like to take a look at it before I leave today. Then I'll change the bandage for you."

"You don't need to bother," the onetime bronc rider said. "It's fine."

"It's not a bother, Nate. That's what I'm here for."

They were a tough lot, those rodeo cowboys. And while Sam had brought on several young and inexperienced hands, Nate had been raised on a ranch. He was also older than the others and seemed like a much better fit.

As Shannon and Blake continued to walk to where she'd parked her car, she again glanced at the gathering clouds.

"Are you worried it's going to rain?" he asked.

"It's supposed to, and I have a long drive back to my apartment in Brighton Valley. So I'd like to get home before it hits. And now would be a good time to leave."

Still, she didn't approach her Toyota Celica, something Blake apparently noticed.

"What's really got you worried?" he asked.

"Sometimes the road near the bridge washes out. So I could have a difficult time getting back tomorrow."

"Does it wash out that easily?"

"No, only when the rain is heavy or constant. But

it does happen." Shannon took her job and responsibility to the ranch seriously. She glanced at Blake,
saw him watching her intently, and lobbed him a
grin. "Maybe it'd be a good idea for you to pack up
your stuff and head back to California before you get
stranded here longer than you planned."

His gaze caressed her face for a moment, which
turned her heart on end. Then his eyes sparked and
his lips quirked into a grin. "I'll risk it."

That didn't sound like the wealthy, career-driven
attorney she'd heard about. She wanted to ask him
to explain himself, to admit why he wanted to hang
out on a struggling cattle ranch/retirement home in
Podunk, Texas. But she supposed it wasn't her business and she opted to hold off with her questions.

She glanced toward the front porch, where a couple of men were sitting—neither of them Rex. Then
she turned back to Blake. His expression, while in-
triguing, was unreadable.

"Thanks for showing me around," he said.

"You're welcome. I needed the fresh air and ex-
ercise." She also enjoyed his company. He could be
pleasant when he wasn't standing up to a perceived
challenge.

"Are you going to have lunch before you go?"
he asked.

"I'm tempted to stay. I love Joy's cooking, but
I have some things to do at home and should also
stop by the dry cleaners. When I got home yesterday, the manager had left me a message, saying I'd
forgotten to pick up a dress I'd dropped off a few
months back."

She probably could have worn it one more time, but it carried the scent of Michael's favorite cologne, reminding her of their last date. The evening had ended in tears—hers. And in her decision to avoid snobs who thought they were better than a "country girl" like her.

So instead of throwing away the expensive dress, just as she'd tossed Michael aside after that disappointing evening spent at a five-star restaurant with his friends, she'd dropped it off at the cleaners instead. She rarely went anywhere that would require her to wear something that fancy, so she hadn't missed it. Besides, ever since starting work at the Rocking Chair Ranch, she hadn't found much need for anything in her closet other than scrubs and jeans.

Shannon stole a glance at Blake, wondering if he thought she was backwards or a novelty of some kind, and caught him studying her as though she'd revealed something about herself and her new life.

"I suppose there's not much chance for you to dress up around here," he said.

He was right about that. And apparently, he was good at connecting dots. "With the time I spend juggling a fifty- or sixty-hour workweek, plus working on the T-bird, there isn't much time for parties or going out on the town."

"That's a shame," he said.

She crossed her arms and arched a brow. "From what I've heard about you, all work and no play makes Blake a dull boy."

"You think so?"

Actually, she had no idea what kind of activities he enjoyed during his spare time, but as their gazes met and locked, a flood of heat warmed her cheeks. Was he flirting with her? It had been so long since someone had that she might be imagining non-existent signs.

Either way, there was no way she'd act upon it. Besides, once she snagged a job at the medical center in Brighton Valley, she'd start making friends and create a new life for herself. God willing, she might even find a man like her father.

"Well," she said, "I'd better not put off those errands. I've got to work again tomorrow."

"Then I'll see you in the morning." He blessed her with a dazzling, heart-strumming smile that only served to weaken her resolve to get on the road.

Were those few chores she planned to do at home all that important?

Would it hurt to wait and stop by the dry cleaners on her next day off? It's not like she had need of that black dress.

Again, she glanced at the sky, trying to gauge just how badly the first storm would hit. Realistically, the road probably wouldn't flood until after a second or third rain.

Before she could consider changing her mind, Alicia Maldonado, the nurse on duty, stepped out the front door and made her way toward Shannon. "I'm glad you're here."

Alicia's olive complexion normally made her look as though she'd just returned from a tropical vacation, but today she was pale, her brown eyes red-rimmed and glossy.

"What's the matter?" Shannon asked.

"I'm not feeling well. It might be something I ate, but if I'm coming down with that virus that's going around, I probably shouldn't be here."

She was right. Doc had given all the residents flu shots, but there was no need to put any of them at risk. "Go on home. I'll cover for you."

"Are you sure you don't want to call in someone else to work this afternoon?" Alicia asked. "You've put in quite a few hours this week already."

Shannon couldn't think of anyone to ask, especially at the last minute. "No, I'm sure. Take care of yourself and get some rest. I'll stay until Darlene gets here this evening." In fact, she'd probably stay longer than that.

The only problem was that whenever she'd spent the night at the Rocking C in the past, she'd slept in Joy's bedroom, which was in the big house. But now that Blake had arrived, Sam was sleeping there. She supposed she'd have to make a bed on the sofa in the office.

As Alicia walked away, Blake said, "It looks like you'll be staying for lunch after all."

"The weatherman has predicted a series of storms coming through. The first one will hit tonight. It might not be all that strong, but since I could have trouble getting in and out of here, it might be best if I don't leave."

"You're going to spend the night?"

That particular question coming from this particular man set off her imagination—and not in a good way. She envisioned a sleepover with the handsome attorney, a slow fire in the hearth, rain pattering softly against the window panes... But there was no way she'd let anything like that happen.

Still, when she glanced at his gorgeous face and saw a glimmer in his eyes that suggested he'd had a similar thought, her hormones soared and her senses reeled. But she quickly roped them all in. Blake wasn't the kind of guy who'd be any more than a passing blip on her radar. She suspected he was a little too much like Michael—and not a thing like her dad.

Don Cramer had been a sweet, gentle soul. An easygoing family man who didn't have a temperamental bone in his body. And Blake Darnell was just the opposite. He'd rise up to any challenge, maybe before one was even made. That probably worked well for him in the courtroom, but it worked against him when dealing with people—especially his uncle.

Shannon, who was a peacemaker at heart, wouldn't want to cross him, but she could be as tough as rawhide when she had to be. If it ever became necessary, she'd go to battle for what was just and right, and she'd do it without a heartbeat's hesitation.

Blake might think of Shannon as a healer, but she was also a fighter when it came to defending the weak, the downtrodden and those she cared about. So if push came to shove, she wouldn't be afraid to go against him.

Hopefully, she wouldn't have to.

The rain began at four o'clock, just a gentle sprinkle at first.

Inside the ranch house, music flowed from the

living room, where a couple of volunteers from the Wexler Junior Women's Club played a variety of music for the residents. They'd brought an Mp3 player, as well as a variety of CDs, mostly vintage country tunes. While the cowboys joined in and turned the small event into a sing-along, Blake had taken the opportunity to go out onto the porch to spend some quiet time to himself—albeit, to the background sound of Willie Nelson singing "Georgia on My Mind."

About an hour earlier, the men who usually sat out here in their rocking chairs on the porch had returned to the house where it was warm and dry. But Blake preferred standing at the railing, looking out at the ranch, listening to the raindrops pelt the roof and watching them fall to the ground. He found it both peaceful and energizing at the same time.

When the screen door creaked open, he turned to see who'd broached his serenity. When he spotted Shannon, a lazy grin slid across his lips.

"Hey," he said. "Aren't you into sing-alongs?"

"Only if there's a karaoke."

"Seriously?" His smile deepened. "You're a wannabe singer?"

"Not really. And only when there are drinks involved." She made her way outside and joined him at the railing. "There was a honky-tonk near our ranch, and sometimes my dad and I liked to go there on Tuesday nights, when they had happy hour prices until closing. Sometimes, when the karaoke started up, we'd sing duets."

Her admission surprised him, and his expression

must have given him away. She crossed her arms, emphasizing not only a bit of annoyance but the fullness of her breasts.

"What's the matter?" she asked. "Does a city boy like you think there's something wrong about having a little fun in a honky-tonk?"

He hadn't meant to suggest any such thing. "Actually, I'm just a little surprised by your...many talents."

As Patsy Cline's bluesy, country voice belted out "Crazy" in the living room, Blake found himself reaching out a hand to Shannon. "Dance with me."

Her eyes widened, and her lips parted. But why wouldn't they? His bold suggestion had taken him by surprise, too.

"Are you...messing with me?"

He wasn't exactly sure what he was doing, but he certainly wasn't teasing her. "I'm just a little caught up in the music." And in the romantic moment.

Shannon waited a beat, then she slipped her hand in his and stepped into his embrace. As they moved together on the porch, the faint scent of her perfume—wildflowers?—taunted him, luring him into a place he'd never been before, a feeling he'd never quite had.

The porch, once rustic and restful, evoked an almost dreamy longing within him. The falling rain created a heavenly veil, enclosing them in a sensual outdoor setting.

The autumn air was cool and crisp, but Shannon's shapely body was warm, fanning a spark that had lain dormant deep in Blake's chest for far too long.

He'd never considered himself to be a romantic, but there was something about the way their bodies moved together and the way their hearts beat in the same rhythm that made the spontaneous dance as mesmerizing and sexy as hell. In spite of his better judgment, he hoped that whatever was flickering between them would go on long after the music ended.

As the song played on, Blake was bombarded with a hodgepodge of emotion, heightened by a growing sense of lust.

A relationship with Shannon, thanks in large part to the distance between them and completely different dreams, was impossible. Yet he couldn't help wondering if she'd consider spending an evening with him.

And sharing more than a dance.

Shannon had no idea why Blake had asked her to slow dance with him on the front porch. Nor did she know why she'd agreed to do it. The whole idea was as crazy as the song implied. He'd told her he was impressed with her talents, which she'd assumed had been sarcastic. After all, he probably frequented fancy clubs in the city, rather than honky-tonks like the Stagecoach Inn.

But for some reason—the way his gaze had locked on hers—she'd felt compelled to take his hand, to step into his arms and to savor the warmth of his muscular frame, the scent of his woodsy cologne.

While the rain poured down around them, creating a cascading wall of water flowing from the eaves, the moment turned romantically surreal. Yet, at the same time, it was incredibly sexy and almost... magical.

But the dance, the intimacy, had to stop. Sharing a romantic moment with Blake Darnell was worse than crazy. Could the two of them be anything other than a match destined to crash and burn before it even got off the ground?

The California attorney was absolutely nothing like the Texas cowboys Shannon had either known or dated in the past, men who valued her and her country life. Sure, he had a solid, muscular build that seemed to have come from hard work. But more likely, it probably came from working out with the weights and equipment at an exclusive Southern California gym he visited regularly, rather than from lifting bales of hay and roping cattle.

And in spite of how well he might fit into those worn jeans that rode low on his narrow hips, he wasn't a man who belonged on a ranch. Instead, he was a city boy through and through, a workaholic who was too consumed with building a lucrative career to find time for his family—or to value a simpler way of life.

He also lived more than a thousand miles away, which meant a relationship between them was completely impossible.

Yet as they swayed to the sensual beat, their bodies fit together so perfectly, and she found herself leaning into him, holding him close, breathing in his musky scent... And, believe it or not, wishing the song would never end.

It would, though. And so would this brief romantic moment.

Shannon really should've pulled away and stopped the stupid dance that was stirring her hormones to a dangerous level and making her weak at the knees, but she couldn't seem to do it. Not when his arms held her close, when his musky scent snaked around her and the sound of the rain pattered on the roof. Who would have guessed that she and Blake could create a harmonious tune of their own?

When the screen door squeaked open and someone stepped out onto the porch, the short-lived spell was broken, and Shannon jerked free of Blake's arms. Her cheeks burned at the thought of being caught in... Well, it wasn't exactly a compromising situation, but she didn't like the idea of someone seeing her and Blake together like this and assuming it meant more than it did.

"What have we here?" Sam asked, a twinkle in his eye and a grin on his lips.

"We just got caught up in the music," Blake said.

Shannon wanted to add, *It's not what you might think*, but she doubted that would convince Sam, especially when he'd recently fallen in love and thought everyone in the world should experience what he had. Besides, she wasn't sure what explanation she could give him for why she'd been dancing with his nephew, especially when she still didn't have an answer herself.

Sam's expression sobered. "I'm sorry to bother you, Shannon, but I'm worried about Rex."

"What's wrong?"

"He came out of his room, pushing his walker, and joined us in the living room. He seemed to be enjoying the music, but he got a phone call from his family and took it in the dining room. When he returned, he looked beat down. I don't know what they said to him, but he went back to his room."

Shannon ran her hands along her denim-clad hips, wishing she'd taken time to change into one of several pairs of clean scrubs she'd packed and brought with her from home. She could certainly use a more professional stance right now, and not just because of Sam's presence. She needed to remind Blake, as well as herself, that she was on duty and not here to...play around.

"I followed him back to his room," Sam said, "and I helped him get into bed. When I asked him what happened, he said he was just tired, which might be true..."

"But...?" Shannon asked.

"I don't think that's the case. He's not doing well, and I'm not just talking about his physical health."

Shannon knew what Sam meant. Rex's brother had died last year, after a lengthy stay in a convalescent hospital, and it still bothered him. Not the old man's loss, but the years leading up to his death. And Shannon certainly understood why it did. That's why she'd promised him she wouldn't let the same thing happen to him—if she could help it.

"I checked on him earlier," Shannon said, "and his vitals were strong. So you're right. That phone call probably upset him. I'll talk to him."

"Thanks," Sam said. "I'd appreciate that."

Checking on Rex also gave her a good excuse to go into the house. She needed to get away from Blake and to shake off the lingering effects of the dance they'd just shared.

If she were to stay outside with him any longer... No, she wasn't even going to think about that.

"If you'll excuse me..." She glanced first at Sam, then at Blake. Without giving either of them a chance to respond, she left them on the porch. She had a job to do, patients to attend to.

And crazy, romantic thoughts would only lead to nowhere fast.

Blake watched Shannon go into the house. When the screen door slapped shut behind her, he turned to his uncle, expecting to see a teasing glimmer in his eye and to have him make a playful comment about the slow dance he'd just witnessed.

Instead, Sam's gaze drilled into him as though Blake had somehow set their relationship back two weeks.

"What's wrong?" he asked.

His uncle folded his arms across his chest. "Rex told me you haven't talked to him yet. When were you going to do that? After his family admits him to some dark and dank convalescent hospital in Arkansas?"

Blake understood Sam's frustration and annoyance. His uncle and Rex were friends, and Sam didn't want to see his old buddy leave the Rocking C, even if it was for his own good.

Bypassing Sam's question altogether and avoiding an apology for not following through on that promised chat as quickly as he should have, Blake took another tack. "Does anyone in his family have power of attorney?"

"Heck, no. Rex would never willingly give any of them that kind of control over him. He'd give it to me first."

"I'm not sure I understand the problem," Blake said. "Is Rex afraid they'll move him against his will?"

"Yep, that's exactly what he's worried about. When his only brother had a stroke six years ago and couldn't talk or put up a fight, they moved him to Arkansas. And Rex doesn't want the same thing to happen to him."

Blake couldn't blame a family for wanting an ailing, elderly relative to be in closer proximity to them. But he didn't want this conversation to morph into something more personal and lead to another argument, so he said, "I realize you're only trying to do what's best for your friend, but if Rex is having health issues, wouldn't it be better if he lived near his family?"

"I can see why you'd make that assumption, but this is different."

Blake couldn't see much difference, although he had to admit that Uncle Sam was doing a heck of a lot better now that he was working on the Rocking C— not just physically, but mentally, too. He'd been only a ghost of a man when Blake had last visited him at the Sheltering Arms.

Poor Sam had really fallen apart when he'd lost Nellie, and understandably so. Nellie had been a wonderful woman, a loving wife—and she'd been one of a kind. That's why it had been such a surprise to learn Sam had replaced her already.

Sam slapped his hands on his hips and cleared his throat. "Will you *please* talk to Rex and tell him you'll put a stop to their harassment?"

Blake didn't think that a few phone calls to the poor old guy could be considered harassment. They might be pressuring him, but it was not as though they could actually force him to move at this point. Either way, he wasn't sure what he could actually do to help.

Sam blew out an exasperated sigh. "I can tell that you've already sided with Rex's family on this, but you don't know the whole story. And if you did, I think you'd agree that Rex has a right to live his own life and to die with his boots on—and right here in Texas."

...a right to live his own life...

I think you'd agree...

Blake knew what his uncle was getting at. Years ago, before college, Blake had harbored a dream to live and work in Texas. He'd gone on to law school at his maternal grandmother's urging, had studied hard and excelled. Once he'd taken the bar exam in Texas and was awaiting the results, she'd insisted he study for the California bar, something he'd been reluctant to do. But she'd paid for him to take a special course for out of state attorneys who wanted to practice in multiple states, insisting it would pay off big for him.

When he passed that exam, too, which hadn't been an easy task, she'd called in a few favors and managed to get him an internship at her investment attorney's firm in Beverly Hills. That position had really opened doors for him, especially since the firm had planned to open an office in Dallas. And now Blake had a successful career, an impressive stock portfolio, a beach house in Malibu and a luxury car with personalized plates.

But there were times when he wished for a quieter life.

"I see your wheels turning," Sam said. "So what have you decided?"

"You have a point," Blake conceded. "Rex does have a right to make his own decisions—at least, while he's still sharp and somewhat healthy. Does he have any significant savings or investments?"

"It always boils down to money for you, doesn't it?" Sam clicked his tongue and scowled. "What does his financial situation have to do with it? Are you planning to charge him for your services?"

This time, it was Blake's turn to bristle. "Of course not. He's your friend. It's just that I wondered if his family was more concerned about his health or his bank account."

"He's got enough to pay for his keep here on the Rocking Chair Ranch."

But was that amount big enough for his greedy relatives to covet?

Blake specialized in estate planning and probate. In the years since he began his practice, he'd seen some pretty nasty family fights over wills. And he knew how death—or one that was imminent—could bring out the worst in people.

That was another reason he worried about his

uncle being swept off his feet by a con artist and why he wanted him to move to California. The fact that he was Sam's only living heir had nothing to do with it. He loved that man and would do anything for him.

Blake placed a hand on his uncle's shoulder and gave it an affectionate squeeze. "I'll talk to Rex tomorrow, okay? I'll also do whatever I can to make sure his family understands his wishes."

"Thanks. I'd appreciate that. And while you're at it, try to understand *my* wishes, too."

Sam was clearly talking about his plan to stay in Texas and to marry another woman.

It would be far more truthful for Blake to say he'd *try* to understand, but he said, "I will."

Sam cast him a smile, gave a slight nod then headed into the house.

Only trouble was, Blake wasn't sure he could follow up on his part of the bargain.

Some wishes weren't meant to come true.

Chapter Six

Blake had assumed the morning sun would awaken him in time to join everyone else at the big house for breakfast, but that hadn't been the case. He just hoped that, when he reached the kitchen, he'd still find some coffee left and maybe a muffin or two.

It had rained hard all night, the thunder and lightning making it difficult to sleep. Fortunately, it had eventually slowed to a drizzle, and he'd finally been able to doze off about an hour before dawn.

Now it was nine o'clock, which was late by ranch standards. So, apparently, he'd been more tired than he'd thought.

As he crossed the yard, he avoided the mud puddles along the pathway by walking on the sopping-wet grass. The sky, which was now dotted with silver-lined clouds, was an amazing shade of blue, something that was rare to see in his smog-ridden big city. He inhaled deeply, filling his lungs with clean, fresh air. Maybe, if the ground dried out, he'd go for an afternoon run.

When he reached the back porch, he scraped the mud from his boots. After wiping them on the mat, he let himself into the house and made his way into the empty kitchen where the aroma of fresh-perked coffee and fried bacon still lingered, long after the last cowboy had eaten breakfast.

The stove and countertops were clean and the breakfast dishes had already been washed and put away. There was no one in sight, but the coffee pot was plugged in and the carafe was half full.

Blake reached into the cupboard, removed a mug and filled it to the brim. He had to admit that Joy was not only an impressive cook, but she also brewed a good pot of java.

He savored several sips before going in search of his uncle's old buddy. He found Rex in the living room, his walker parked nearby. He wore a pair of glasses and was reading a book, the lamp next to him bathing the words in light.

"Hey, there," Blake said. "Is this a good time for us to talk?"

"As good a time as any." The old cowboy dog-eared the page he'd been reading, removed his glasses and set them and the novel on the small oak table beside him. "Sam told me you were a sharp lawyer and that you'd be able to help me."

"I can try." Blake spotted a wooden chair by the

hearth and, taking care not to spill the coffee from his mug, carried it closer to Rex and took a seat. "Why don't you start by telling me what's going on?"

"All-righty." Rex sat back in his easy chair and rested his liver-spotted hands on the armrests, his fingers folding over the edge. "I'll be eighty-three years old in December. I've had a good life, but I'm not in the best of health, so I know which way the wind is blowing. I'm not going to live forever, which is okay by me. All I want to do is die with my boots on and be buried in the Twin Falls Cemetery, next to my sweet wife—God rest her soul. Is that too much to ask?"

"No," Blake said. "That sounds reasonable."

"Good. Then I'd like for you to use all of your legal jargon to tell that to the misguided do-gooders in my family. I want them to stop butting in to my life and trying to force their beliefs and opinions on me."

"How are they 'butting in' and pressuring you?" Blake asked.

"They plan to haul my ass to Arkansas and put me in that same damn convalescent hospital where my brother was left to rot until the day he died."

"And you're afraid they'll just leave you there until you pass?"

Rex snorted. "Worse than that. They'd do their best to keep me breathing, even at the cost of my dignity."

"I'm not sure I'm following you," Blake said.

Rex leaned forward and narrowed a tired but feisty gaze at Blake. "They kept my poor brother hooked up on machines for the last four miserable years of his existence." Rex lifted a gnarled finger and gave it a threatening shake. "And I ain't gonna just roll over and let them do the same to me. Besides, I'm a cowboy. I belong here—on a ranch and in Texas. And this is where I intend to stay."

"Just for the record," Blake said, "you can get a medical directive that puts your feelings in writing."

"Yeah, well what if that paperwork gets lost—or hidden? I don't trust them do-gooders."

"If it's in your file at the Rocking C, it will follow you to the hospital."

"You sure about that?"

Blake nodded. The problem was that someday Rex might require long-term medical treatment in a hospital setting. And he wasn't going to like that, whether he was living in Texas or Arkansas. Especially if he didn't have the right paperwork in place to protect his interests.

"For the record," Blake said, "I can understand why you'd prefer to stay on the Rocking Chair Ranch."

Rex eyed him carefully, as if gauging his sincerity.

"The food they serve here is pretty damn good," Blake added, hoping to convince the oldster that he was on his side—at least, somewhat. "And from what I hear, the nursing care is excellent."

Rex grinned. "You got that right. Since Doc convinced me that I shouldn't live alone anymore, this is the next best place to be. I might not be able to rope and ride like I used to, but I can still sit out on the porch and spin yarns with my old friends. And I can advise those young cowhands Sam hired, which sure beats the hell out of parking my scrawny butt on a bench in some hospital rose garden and hoping the pigeons don't crap on me."

Blake couldn't help but grin. No wonder Shannon liked Rex. He might be crotchety, but he was full of life, that was for sure.

"On top of that," Rex said, "the folks who live and work on the Rocking C are a hell of a lot more like family to me than the ones I have."

That said a lot. Blake just hoped the old cowboy's health would hold up and he wouldn't have to move at all.

"And how 'bout that head nurse?" Rex asked, his tired brown eyes sparking with mirth. "She's a pretty one—and as kind and sweet as they come, although I 'spect she could really get riled up if someone pushed her."

"I 'spect you're right," Blake said, falling right back into the cowboy vernacular he'd loved listening to when he was a kid.

"She's got a heart for the sick and wounded, and while I have no idea what we'd do without her, I know that she'd much rather have a position at the hospital in town. Her skills would probably be a whole lot more useful there, but as a favor to Chloe, the woman who owns this place, she's filling in temporarily."

Shannon had said as much to Blake. So it appeared that he'd been wrong about her intending to take advantage of the cowboys.

"She also managed to get Joy a job working here," Rex added, "and that turned out to be a win-win for everyone. Boy, howdy, that gal can cook."

"You're right. She sure whips up some mighty fine grub." There he went again, talking like one of the ranch hands, but it was hard not to when he'd been living with them for the past few days.

"It's too bad what happened to her," Rex said.

"To *who*? Joy?"

"Yep. Her first husband set her up nicely, leaving her a tidy little nest egg and house in a Dallas suburb that was fully paid for. But after he up and died on her, she remarried a louse of a man who talked her into refinancing her home and taking out all the equity. Before she knew it, that no-good son of a bitch spent it all and drained her savings account, too, and the property went into foreclosure. Then he ran off with another grieving widow, leaving Joy not only dead broke, but with no place to live. Fortunately, her job here provides her with room and board."

Blake hadn't realized Joy had been homeless and destitute before coming to the Rocking C. Had he been right all along? Had she turned her charms on Sam to save herself from a desperate situation?

"But Joy's walkin' in tall cotton now," Rex said.

Blake tensed. "How so?"

"Who would have guessed that a romance would spark between her and Sam?" Rex chuckled. "That lucky dog."

Blake didn't think Sam was lucky. Dammit, the situation was worse than he'd thought.

"What's the matter?" Rex asked. "You look like a little kid who's just had his bicycle snatched by a bully. Don't tell me your uncle's new romance is bothering you."

Was it that obvious?

"I'd think that you'd be happy about his new lease on life," Rex said, "especially since he pert near died in that so-called skilled nursing facility six months ago. You saw what happened to him there. He sank into a depression and lost about thirty pounds. Even his doctor had been about to quit on him and turn him over to those hospice folks."

"Yes, I know." Blake had to admit that going back to work on the Rocking C had helped Sam make a full recovery, although who knew how long a man nearing eighty years old could continue running a ranch, especially one that was struggling financially.

"Chloe used to work at that hospital," Rex added, "and thanks to her care and friendship, your uncle began to perk up and come around. Then, after he got here and settled in, Joy showed up. Her smile and cooking soon turned the tide."

Blake was happy to see Sam doing well. It was just that he didn't want to see him hurt—emotionally, mentally or financially. "I'm glad Sam isn't drowning in his grief anymore. It's just that he loved my aunt and seems to have forgotten her already."

She's gone, son, Sam had told him. *And I was heartsick when she passed. But don't I deserve to be happy again?*

Yes, he did. But Blake had made the mistake of proposing to Melissa without really getting to know her first. And he soon learned that she valued the things he could buy her more than she valued him.

"Sam hasn't forgotten your aunt," Rex said. "I can guarantee that. Heck, I still dream of the days when my Jenny was alive, when we were young and still had a lot of good years ahead of us. Some men aren't fortunate enough to ever find that kind of love. But Sam's found it twice."

Blake hoped Rex was right, but he wasn't convinced, especially now that he knew Joy had been broke and homeless before she hooked up with Sam.

"You look doubtful." Rex chuckled. "I 'spect that's because you haven't found your own true love yet. Don't worry about your uncle. He'll be fine. And whether my family knows it or not, I will be, too. If there's one thing I hate, it's for people to think a man's not worth his salt because he's beyond his prime. They'd just as soon put us all out to pasture, but if my Arkansas kin want to do that to me, I'll go down swinging."

Blake didn't doubt that.

"If you take anything away from our little chit-chat," Rex said, "wrap your head around this: Sam hasn't forgotten Nellie at all. He only forgot the ache of losing her."

Blake hoped that was true.

"Oh, and one more thing." A glimmer in the old man's eyes shaved a couple of years off his craggy face. "If you know what's good for you, you'll start scouting around for a good woman, one like Jenny, Nellie or Joy."

Blake might consider that—assuming there was one out there for him. Without any effort on his part, his thoughts drifted to Shannon, just as her voice sounded behind him.

"I hope I'm not interrupting anything," she said.

Blake turned to the pretty RN, who was wearing a pair of sky blue scrubs and a smile. She was also carrying a tray with a glass of water and a small paper cup that probably held medication.

Her bright eyes tugged at something deep inside of Blake, setting off a tingling sensation that swept through his belly like a swarm of butterflies in flight.

As if unaware of any effect she'd had on him, she turned her focus on Rex. "It's good to see you out and about again. And I'm glad you're using that walker instead of your cane."

Blake watched and listened to her cajole Rex into taking his pills. Afterward, she took his blood pressure and listened to his heart. All the while, she was sweet and gentle, and her smile never faded. It was actually something to watch her dole out a little TLC that the old man surely needed.

Shannon was not only a pleasure on the eyes, she appeared to be a good-hearted woman, the kind of woman his uncle said Blake would find one day.

He actually found himself hoping she was, although time would tell—time he was limited to when it came to his stay in Texas.

By afternoon, dark clouds had moved in to cover the blue sky that had amazed Blake earlier. Still, he'd gone for a long, hard run. When he returned to the small outbuilding in which he'd been staying, he called the office, using the landline since his cell didn't always work.

Carol gave him a rundown of the status of his pending cases, as well as the motions that had been served. Everything seemed to be going okay, at least so far.

"So how's your uncle doing?" she asked.

"He looks good," Blake admitted. "But I'm still worried about him." He went on to explain why and was glad she didn't quiz him further. Carol was aware of his initial concern, so he didn't need to go on about it too much.

"Are you enjoying your time away from the office?" she asked.

"Surprisingly, yes. It's been peaceful, so I've gotten some much-needed rest. I even had a good run today."

"I'm glad to hear that. Are you ready for me to book your return flight?"

When he'd first arrived at the ranch, he'd been eager to talk some sense into Sam and to quickly take him back to LA. But convincing Sam to leave wasn't going to be easy now. And thanks to that talk he'd had with Rex earlier, Blake wasn't entirely sure that he ought to even try.

Of course, that didn't mean he wanted to see that romance continue, especially if Sam suffered a breakup like the one Blake had with Melissa.

"No," he told Carol. "I'm not ready to book any flights—unless you think I'm needed back at the office."

"I won't lie to you," the administrative assistant said. "Your absence has added to everyone's workload. But they all understand."

Two weeks ago, before he'd received those legal documents from Sam's Texas attorney, he wouldn't have considered leaving the office in a lurch. And while his conscience wasn't feeling too keen about it now, he wasn't going to rush back.

"Thanks for laying it on the line," he told Carol. "I'll get back to you in a day or so once I know my plans."

After the call ended, Blake headed to the big house. It would be mealtime soon, and he'd eaten a light lunch because of his planned run.

When he entered the mudroom, he spotted his uncle speaking to Joy while she stood at the counter, cutting out biscuits and lining them on a baking pan.

"If it isn't raining in the morning," Sam was saying to her, "let's drive into Brighton Valley after breakfast and talk to Ralph Nettles."

At least Sam hadn't referred to the guy as "Pastor Ralph," so it didn't sound as if they were planning a wedding or attending pre-marital counseling. Still, his curiosity was piqued. "Who's Ralph Nettles?"

When Sam furrowed his brow and shot him a frown, he realized he shouldn't have asked, since the original question hadn't been directed to him. But tell that to his overblown concern about his uncle's future plans.

"Ralph is a Realtor," Sam said. "He's going to show us some houses."

Blake's chest cramped. Sam was really going to do it then. He was going to purchase a house for Joy. As nice as she'd been to Blake, and as much as he enjoyed her meals, he couldn't let that sway him. And while he was glad to see his uncle smiling again, he couldn't help fearing that after Joy got the deed to a new house in hand, she'd leave Sam in the dust.

Besides, Joy was still young enough to find another man. And at Sam's age, he could end up having health issues that would require her to have to nurse him at the end.

He hoped Joy was in this thing for the duration—for richer or poorer, in sickness and in health—until death parted them. But how could he be sure?

As he studied his uncle's smile, the way his eyes twinkled when he gazed at the ranch cook, Blake realized the old man's emotions would be dashed when Joy decided to leave.

Sure, the woman might be genuine. But why would she expect Sam to buy her a house, to fix her teeth or to send her niece to medical school? And where was this niece? Was she even sharp enough to be accepted to med school in the first place?

He'd had a wait-and-see attitude, but he couldn't stay in Texas indefinitely. He needed to go back to the office. Maybe he ought to push things a bit, test Joy's character to make sure she was the kind of woman who wasn't just in it for the money—and that she'd be willing to stick by Sam's side when the going got tough.

If there was one thing Blake had learned from his maternal grandparents, it was that money could buy just about anything. And for that reason, it could also buy off just about anyone.

"Supper is almost ready," Joy told Blake. "But in the meantime, would you like a glass of sweet tea? Or maybe some cheese and crackers to tide you over?"

"The tea sounds good, but I'll wait and eat with everyone else."

"I'd better check on the hands and tell them to wash up." Sam gave Joy an affectionate kiss.

Would Blake ever get used to seeing the couple so lovey-dovey? Or better yet, would he even have to?

After Sam went outside, Joy handed Blake an ice-cold glass of tea. "Are you sure I can't get you anything else?"

"No, thanks." He made his way to the big oak table, which had already been set for the young cowboys and Sam. He leaned his hip against one of the chairs. "I'd actually like to talk to you if you have a minute."

"Sure," she said. "Let me just put the biscuits in the oven."

When she'd done that, she turned to face him, wearing a smile. It was a warm one that said, "Let's be friends." But Blake couldn't let himself be as easily charmed by it as his uncle had been.

Even before he asked the question, a niggle of guilt rose up in his chest, suggesting he might be overstepping. But he squashed it down and pressed on. "What would you say if I asked how much it would take for you to let my uncle down easily and move on to someone else who could take on your financial woes?"

Her expression shifted from sweet to shocked to crushed, transforming that niggle of guilt to a giant-sized feeling of shame.

Tears welled in her eyes, and she tried to blink them back without much success. "It's…not like that.

You're...wrong." Her voice cracked, the hurt apparent, even to a hard-hearted fool—and right now, Blake felt like the worst kind.

Before he could apologize or explain that he'd only been testing her, a test she seemed to have passed, Shannon entered the kitchen.

"Something sure smells good," the nurse said, her voice upbeat and cheery. But when she glanced at Joy, when she spotted the tears running down her cheeks, all signs of cheerfulness dissipated into the air.

"What's wrong?" Her gaze flitted from Joy to Blake and back again.

"Nothing." Joy sniffled, then reached for a paper towel to blot her eyes and her nose. "Please...excuse me." Then she hurried out of the room.

Shannon turned to face Blake, anger blazing in her eyes. "I'm not buying that. What did you say to her?"

Since Joy was so obviously crushed by the offer, she must care more for Sam than Blake had realized. And that being said, he'd have to address her hurt feelings, something that unbalanced him. He'd never been very good at handling tears.

Of course, he also had Shannon to deal with. She was glaring at him like a little bantam hen, ready to fight anyone in the barnyard who'd dare to challenge or threaten one of her chicks.

"There's been a little misunderstanding." *Nice one, Darnell. The only misunderstanding was your own when you misjudged Joy's motives and went out on a scrawny limb by offering to buy off her feelings—which just might be the real deal.*

Apologies didn't come easy. The one Blake had

offered Sam had been sincere and necessary, but it had been a rough one to make. And when Sam heard about this… Oh, damn. Blake had really stepped in it now. Sam was going to hit the roof.

"I screwed up," he said, "I made an assumption and said something to her that I shouldn't have said. So I owe her an apology."

The anger in Shannon's eyes had died down, but he doubted it would take much to flare up again.

"What did you say to her?"

"I…" This was going to make him sound like an ass, even to himself. "I offered her money to let Sam down easily."

"Are you kidding me? That was a cruel and thoughtless thing for you to do. What kind of man are you?"

One who was only trying to look after his uncle's best interests, but he'd clearly stepped over the line and wasn't sure how to backpedal.

"I'm sorry for assuming the worst," he admitted. "Joy is an amazing cook who's provided the men here with the kind of homemade meals they've probably been missing for years. And she's apparently made my uncle happy. I didn't mean to suggest that she didn't have real feelings for him. It's just that things seemed to happen so fast that I was confused by it all. I just… I just…" Blake blew out a battered breath. "I know there are women out there who are more interested in what a man can provide for them than in the man himself."

Shannon crossed her arms and arched a single brow. "Oh, do you."

He wasn't about to spill his guts, to let her know how disappointed he'd been when he'd walked in on Melissa talking to one of her friends about the big house she was going to insist Blake buy, the expensive car she'd soon be driving around town, the whopping big diamond she'd soon be sporting.

Melissa's dishonesty had done a real number on him. But then again, even his mother had made it no secret that she appreciated the finer things in life more than she had Blake's late father.

"Believe it or not," he said, "I've experienced women like that myself. But I made the wrong assumption this time, and I'll figure out a way to make things right."

Shannon didn't respond, and by her expression, he realized she hadn't softened a bit. Instead, she glared at him as if he'd really made a mess of things. And apparently, the head nurse wasn't going to be nearly as forgiving and understanding as he'd hoped she'd be. And that bothered him a lot more than he cared to admit.

"I'll apologize to Joy," he said.

Yet, for some reason, it seemed to be Shannon's forgiveness he needed.

Chapter Seven

For a woman who'd once had a quick temper, Shannon prided herself on being able to keep it in check these days. But Blake's audacity had caused her to nearly lose her grip.

When Blake had first arrived at the Rocking C, he'd been strung as tight as a war drum and ready for battle. She'd heard that he was a hard-nosed negotiator, but his attitude that day had still surprised and annoyed her.

Recently, she'd begun to see his sweeter side, as well as a playfulness that had drawn her to him. So she'd begun to think they might actually become friends. In fact, after their dance on the porch, she'd even entertained a few romantic thoughts about him, about *them*. But that was before he'd made such a false assumption and cruel comment about her aunt's character.

Joy was one of the kindest, gentlest souls Shannon had ever known, and it crushed her to see her aunt in tears.

"What's the matter?" Blake asked. "I'm going to tell her I'm sorry."

"Knowing Joy, she'll forgive you. But I guess you could say that I don't turn the other cheek as easily as she does."

Blake eyed her carefully, but not critically. No, his expression seemed more stunned and surprised.

"I understand why Joy was hurt," he said. "But why are you taking this personally?"

For a lot of reasons, only one of which was her relationship to Joy, a woman she'd defend to her dying day. But another was because she'd lowered her guard around Blake.

If truth be told, she'd actually wanted to believe that he'd inherited many of Sam's traits, but she wasn't about to voice that pointless wish. So she said, "I don't like seeing people upset, especially my employees."

At that point, Shannon nearly pulled the relative card and told Blake that she would defend and protect her aunt until her dying day, but she'd do the same for any of the people who lived or worked on the Rocking C. So why let him think her disappointment in him was "personal" when it was just a matter of common courtesy, understanding and respect?

"I was wrong to make that offer to her," Blake said. "The only explanation I have is that I don't want to see Sam hurt. He's already lost the love of his life, which nearly killed him. And I..." He paused, then slowly shook his head, apparently thinking a further explanation wasn't necessary.

And maybe it wasn't. Shannon shifted her weight to one hip. "I don't want to see either one of them brokenhearted. And it irritates me to think that you'd assume the woman who's been cooking your meals, treating you kindly and doing her best to make sure you feel welcome around here would take the money you offered her and run."

His eye twitched ever so slightly. Then he shrugged a single shoulder. "It's been known to happen. Some women aren't what they seem."

"Yeah, well, that offer you just made to Joy tells mc a lot about the kind of man *you* really are."

"Touché," he said, his voice humbled, his expression contrite.

Shannon wanted to hang on to her anger and throw a few more accusations his way, but she decided to let it go—at least, for now. Besides, she'd made her point, and he'd admitted that he'd been wrong.

"So what can I do to makc it up to you?" he asked.

"I suppose you could try to be more like your uncle and less of an insensitive jerk."

He seemed to chew on that for a second or two, then a slow grin slid across his face, making him far more appealing to her at the moment than he should be. "I'm probably more like my uncle than you think. He's got a protective streak, too."

"Yes, I've seen it. But he's not one to hurt someone's feelings unless they really deserve it."

Again, he studied her. "I suspect Sam is going to hear about this and jump all over my case."

"You'd be deserving of it."

"Maybe you're right."

There was no "maybe" about it, but she wasn't as eager to see him get his comeuppance as she'd been just minutes ago.

Blake nodded toward the doorway to the service porch. "I'd better find Sam and tell him what I said before Joy does."

After chugging down the last of his tea, Blake rinsed the glass and left it in the sink. Then he headed outside, shoulders slumped ever so slightly.

As the door shut behind him, Shannon felt a strange compulsion to go after him, to be a buffer between him and his uncle.

She didn't, of course. But for a moment, she actually wanted to defend and protect Blake, too.

Blake found his uncle in the barn, wearing a tool belt and heading out to the yard.

"Got a minute?" he asked.

Sam's steps slowed. "Sure. What's up?"

Blake expected all hell to break loose when he told his uncle what he'd done, but Sam merely shook his head and said, "Damn fool kid. What in the hell am I going to do with you?"

Sam's disgust and disappointment packed a gut-wrenching wallop to Blake's solar plexus, something he hadn't felt since he was sixteen and had borrowed the ranch pickup without permission. He'd met up with some friends at the ball field that day, but on the way home, while adjusting the volume on the radio and not watching the road, he'd taken out a couple of mailboxes and nearly run the truck into a ditch. He'd hoped his deed would go unnoticed, but he couldn't hide the cracked windshield and dented hood. Needless to say, Sam had hit the roof.

If Blake had thought Joy's tears had been hard to handle just minutes ago, the loss of Sam's respect was even worse now.

"This isn't an excuse," Blake said, knowing how Sam felt about people making them after they'd screwed-up. "But do you remember Melissa Bennett?"

"That redhead with dollar signs in her eyes?"

"That's the one." Blake was surprised at his uncle's perceptiveness. He'd introduced Melissa to Sam and Nellie a year and a half ago, when he'd taken her to visit them after they moved to the Sheltering Arms. But he'd never discussed the details of their breakup. "How did you know she had...a greedy side?"

"Because she kept noticing things like that two-karat diamond ring I bought your aunt on our fiftieth wedding anniversary and the Waterford crystal in the hutch. And on top of that, she didn't seem to give a rip about the photos of you and your dad that Nellie had framed and displayed on the wall. When I pointed out a couple of them, like the ones of you riding Chester for the very first time or holding that line of trout we caught at the Founder's Day Picnic at Riley's Creek, she just glossed over them to look at Nellie's collection of Lladró figurines."

Blake wished he'd noticed what his aunt and uncle had spotted in Melissa sooner. It would have saved him a lot of grief later. He glanced at Sam, whose expression had softened a bit. "I'm not sure how I missed seeing that."

"Because you were looking at her through your hormones and not your brain."

"Why didn't you say something?" Blake asked.

"Would you have listened to me? Or to *anyone*? Some people need to learn about life the hard way, Blake. But if it makes you feel any better, your father didn't like taking advice about matters of the heart, either."

"You mean when it came to dating my mother?"

Sam nodded. "I knew that relationship wasn't going to work the first time he brought your mom to the ranch. I tried to tell him why, but he wouldn't listen."

Blake knew what Sam meant. His parents had met in college, but they hadn't been a good match, mostly because their backgrounds had been so different. His dad had been raised by Sam and Nellie, who'd loved and cherished him as their own. They'd also taught him a good, solid work ethic.

On the other hand, Blake's mother had been coddled as a child and used to getting her way, so their marriage was troubled from the start.

He might have only been a kid at the time his dad died, but he'd lived with his parents, heard their constant arguments and suspected a divorce was on the horizon. Looking back, he realized his maternal grandfather had managed to keep them together by sending them on a cruise, buying them a new car or... on that fateful weekend, springing for a vacation in Vail.

Sam lifted his Stetson and raked his hand through

his hair. "I came to the conclusion that a man's got to make his own decisions about women, even if he ends up making a big mistake."

"You're probably right. About six months after I introduced you to Melissa, I finally saw the dollar signs in her eyes and realized she was only using me for the life she thought I'd provide her."

"I figured you would see through her facade— eventually. I'm just glad you didn't marry her."

"Me, too. But thanks to her, I'm skeptical about a woman's motives. So when you mentioned house hunting with Joy, I was afraid she might be…playing you."

"Like that snooty redhead tried to play you?" Sam huffed, then readjusted his hat on his head. "Open your heart, son. If you do, you'll see that Joy doesn't have a greedy bone in her body."

Blake hoped his uncle was right. He glanced toward the house, expecting to see Joy slip outside, hurry to the barn, sidle up to Sam and tell him how badly Blake had hurt her feelings.

But that never happened. Instead, she remained indoors, keeping to herself—at least for now.

Was she that interested in preserving family peace and harmony?

Apparently, Sam and Shannon both thought that she was, and maybe they were right.

"Don't worry," Blake told his uncle. "From now on I'll stay out of your business and treat Joy with the respect she deserves."

"I'll hold you to your word," Sam said. "I assume you apologized to her."

"I'm going to—as soon as I see her."

"Good. I'm glad to hear that." Sam placed a hand on Blake's shoulder, gripping it with a solid but gentle strength, just the way he used to offer his guidance to Blake years ago. "I know you're worried about me making a mistake, but trust me, I'm not. I'm in love with Joy and, whether you like it or not, I'm going to marry her. It'd just make my life a lot easier and happier if you'd try to accept her. But that's your call."

Blake nodded his agreement, although he wasn't sure how he was going to fit into the new Darnell family dynamics.

"Now, if you'll excuse me," Sam said, "I've got to go check on Nate and the other hands. That poor guy has his hands full trying to help me teach the youngsters how to be decent cowboys."

As Sam walked out into the yard, Blake toyed with the idea of leaving Texas and heading back to Los Angeles, which was probably for the best.

He scanned the barn one last time, breathing in the dusty scent of straw, horses and leather. Then he headed to the house to find Joy, after which he planned to call Carol at the office.

The kitchen was empty, which meant he'd have to search for Joy—or wait for her to return.

In the meantime, he crossed the room to the old-style telephone on the wall, picked up the receiver and dialed the familiar number. When Carol answered, he said, "I'm ready for you to book my return flight—but only mine. Let me know what my options are."

"Will do."

While Blake waited, he poured himself a cup of

coffee, snatched a banana from the fruit bowl on the counter and took a seat at the table.

Five minutes later, Carol returned his call with several possible itineraries. "The earliest flight I can schedule out of Houston is tomorrow morning," she said. "But there are two more in the afternoon and one in the evening. Will any of those work for you?"

"Keep in mind that I have a two-to-three-hour drive to Houston." If he wanted to catch a morning flight, he'd need to leave tonight.

Only problem was, he'd come here to mend fences and had almost succeeded—until he'd damn near torn them down again. He wouldn't feel right about leaving until he apologized to Joy and was sure he'd really patched things up with Sam. Or at least, knowing that he'd given it his best shot.

But this time, he didn't just need to make peace with his uncle. He'd have to get on a better footing with Joy, too. She might accept his apology, but something told him that wasn't going to be enough. At least, not for Sam.

And, truthfully, not for Blake.

To make matters even more complicated, he wanted to fix things between him and Shannon, too.

As an attorney, he faced conflict every day and sometimes had people unhappy with him for various reasons. He always managed to shake it off and get on with life. But this was different.

Shannon was different. Her smile had the power to set his heart soaring, and knowing he'd given her a bad impression of him left him unsettled.

He had to do something to remedy that. But what?

He'd already told her he'd been out of line and that he was sorry for it. But she hadn't completely forgiven him, and he needed to do more. He had to get on her better side, even if it was just to see her smile again, to hear her laugh.

He wasn't quite sure where to start, but if there was one thing Blake had learned from his maternal grandfather, it's that a man put his money where his mouth—and where his heart—was.

"You know," he told Carol, "tomorrow is a little too soon. Can you try to get that ticket for two days from now?"

"You bet. I'll let you know what's available."

After he ended the call, he pondered all the possible ways he could fix things, the gifts and peace offering he could make. Hopefully, the next two days on the Rocking C would give him enough time to make things right.

And to see Shannon smile at him again.

Shannon carried out a tray of cookies to the men, stopping first to offer one to Rex, who was reading in the living room.

"Is that a good book?" she asked.

"Not bad. I've read it before, but I'm a big fan of Louis L'Amour." He marked his page, then set the paperback aside on the lamp table next to him. "That guy sure knows how to tell a good story."

She lowered the tray, which held several small paper plates that each bore a couple of freshly baked chocolate chip cookies. "Would you like a snack? They're fresh from the oven and still warm."

"Thanks." Rex took one of the plates and placed it on the table, next to his book. But rather than snatch one of the cookies, he let them sit there.

"Aren't you hungry?" she asked.

"Not really. I'm not feeling too frisky today. In fact, I was just thinking about heading back to my room for a nap. But now that you're here, I have a question for you."

"What's that?"

"You know that paper I signed? The one that says I don't want to be put on life support?"

"The DNR," she said. "Yes, what about it?"

"If I ever have to go to a hospital—God forbid, and believe me, I'll fight you tooth and nail every step of the way—do you promise that paper will go with me? I don't want my relatives getting ahold of it and tossing it out so they can claim it doesn't exist."

"Don't worry. It's in your medical file, which will follow you wherever you go."

"That's what Sam's nephew said, but I wanted to double-check with you."

The screen door creaked open, and when Shannon turned to see who'd entered the house, she spotted Blake holding a couple bouquets of yellow roses and what appeared to be a box of chocolates.

"Well, speak of the devil," Rex said. "Here's my lawyer now."

A grin tugged at Blake's lips, and he made his way toward them. "What'd I do this time?"

"From the looks of those flowers and that candy," Rex said, "you're either sweet on a lady or you ruffled her feathers."

"My guess is that he's making a peace offering to our cook," Shannon said. "She already accepted his apology, but the flowers and chocolate are a nice follow-up gesture."

"I hope so," Blake said. "Is Joy in the kitchen?"

"Yes, she was just starting to fix the evening meal."

Blake glanced at the tray Shannon held, and his grin widened. "Looks like I got here just in time. Maybe, after I give her flowers, she'll let me have a cookie, too."

"I'm sure she will." Shannon couldn't help returning his smile. Blake might be a jerk at times, but at least he wasn't above making an apology when he realized one was in order.

After he carried the roses and chocolate to the kitchen, Shannon passed out treats to the other cowboys. Then she returned to the main part of the house with the empty tray.

Rex was still seated near the lamp, his expression pensive. The book he'd been reading now rested on the table beside him, and he hadn't touched his cookies.

"Is something wrong?" she asked.

"No, but I'm tuckered out. I think I'll make my way back to my room now."

"Here." Shannon reached out her free hand to assist him in getting out of the chair.

Rex waved her off, pulled his walker close and gripped the handles. "I don't need any help."

She was about to argue, knowing that he wasn't nearly as strong and stable as he wanted her to think he was, but she held her tongue. Rex had a lot of pride. Still, she remained beside him, prepared to help him if he stumbled.

Once he'd gotten to his feet, he looked at her and winked. "See? I got it."

But as she watched him head down the hall to his room, his head bent, his steps slow, her heart ached for him.

"Oh, good," Blake said, from behind her. "You're still here."

She turned to the sound of his voice and spotted him holding a single bouquet.

He crossed the living room floor and handed her the yellow roses. "I thought I'd better try to make amends with you, too."

The gesture took her aback, but she thanked him and took the plastic-wrapped spray. Unable to resist, she lifted the blooms to her nose, took a whiff of their fragrance, then said, "You didn't have to do this."

"I know, but I wanted to. I also spotted a small Italian restaurant near the flower stand. I know you enjoy Joy's meals, but I thought you'd like a change of pace this evening. What do you say about having dinner with me before I head back to California?"

The suggestion, which sounded a whole lot like a date, was completely unexpected, yet it also intrigued her. Whether he knew it or not, ever since moving to town and taking this position, she hadn't done anything more exciting in the evening than cuddling up on the sofa alone and watching a movie on Netflix.

"What's the matter?" he asked. "Don't you want to have dinner with me?"

"No, it's not that…" Actually, for some dumb reason the idea appealed to her, but she probably ought to graciously decline.

"I'm going home in a couple of days, and I hate the idea of leaving you with bad memories of me." His eyes, which were the color of the Texas sky, sparked with...something. She couldn't exactly put her finger on just what she saw there, but whatever it was, it shot across the room in a jagged, lightning-fast arc, jolting her heart like a tiny, invisible defibrillator.

"That sounds nice," she said, "but it isn't necessary for you to take me out."

Darn it. That sounded as if she thought his friendly gesture was supposed to be a date. And that's surely not what he'd meant it to be.

"I owe it to you," he said. "Do you like Italian food?"

Actually, she loved it. But she would have been tempted to go with him, even if he'd suggested they eat at that rundown diner near the truck stop. "I'm just reluctant to leave..."

"Isn't Darlene coming tonight? Can't she cover for you?"

"Yes, but it might rain again, before we get back. And if the bridge washes out, we'll be stuck. Worse than that, if any of the residents needed medical care, and I'm not here to provide it, they'd probably have to call in Life Flight."

That playful spark in his eye dimmed, and something else took its place. Disappointment, maybe?

No, not that... Shannon tightened her grip on both the flowers and the dangling tray. "What's the matter?"

"I guess I didn't realize how bad things could get in the valley in bad weather." His smile returned, although it bore a serious slant. "But I admire you for how seriously you take your job."

The compliment, especially coming from him, warmed her to the bone. But she forced herself to shrug off the praise. "I'm all they have around here, especially when the creek rises. Even Doc Nelson lives on the far side of the bridge."

"Then maybe we ought to go out for an early dinner, before it starts to rain."

Going out with Blake, whether it was a real date or not, was sounding better and more feasible every minute. The only problem was, she really didn't have anything to wear. That black dress was still at the cleaners, and she hadn't brought too many optional outfits with her. She certainly wasn't going to wear her scrubs.

"How fancy is that place?" she asked.

"It's just a hole in the wall, but it looks decent on the outside. I spotted a lot of cars parked in front, which is always a good sign."

She bit down on her bottom lip and tried to come up with a good reason to thank him for the offer and tell him no. But when he reached out and cupped her cheek, her breath caught and she couldn't seem to form a sensible thought or utter a single word.

As his gaze locked on hers, a bevy of pheromones surged inside her. And when his thumb stroked her cheek, a wave of heat shot right through her, melting her heart.

Every excuse she might have given failed to take shape. As a result, her only response was a nod.

Chapter Eight

Papa Giovanni's, which boasted a mural of Venice on the far wall, wasn't the kind of restaurant Blake usually frequented, nor would it be considered the least bit fancy. It was just a small dining room, with red checkered tablecloths, white paper place mats and plastic-covered menus.

If this particular eatery was located in Beverly Hills, the prices would have garnered a single $ on Yelp or any other review websites. But the hearty aroma of tomatoes, basil and garlic, as well as fresh baked bread, provided Blake with the only rating he needed to know he'd made a good choice.

He hadn't considered his time out with Shannon to be a date, but that belief changed the moment she'd met him in the Rocking C living room wearing a pair of tight black jeans and a cream-colored sweater, both of which showed off her sexy curves.

As he'd gazed at her, a slew of compliments jammed in his throat, making it nearly impossible to comment on her stunning appearance. One of the cowboys, who'd been watching a game show on TV, took one look at her and blew out an appreciative whistle.

Jumping on the oldster's cue, Blake winked at the man and said, "You've got that right, buddy."

Shannon had smiled, and her cheeks flushed a pretty shade of pink.

Now she and Blake were seated across from each other in a darkened corner booth, the bulk of the light coming from a drippy red candle stuck in an empty Chianti bottle. Yet this evening was already far more romantic than any of the nights he'd spent with Melissa in five-star restaurants.

The difference had nothing to do with the setting and everything to do with the woman he was with, the lovely, kindhearted nurse with lush dark curls tumbling over her shoulders and expressive green eyes glimmering as she glanced up from her menu. When she smiled, the romantic aura morphed into one that was sexually charged.

Before he could consider what he wanted to do about it—if anything—a balding middle-aged man wearing an apron approached the table.

"Can I get you something to drink?" he asked.

"Yes," Blake told the guy who appeared to be their waiter, as well as the chef. Then he asked Shannon if she'd like to start with a glass of wine.

"That sounds good."

Blake turned back to the waiter. "Then we'll have a bottle of your best red wine."

The man brightened. "It's a Valpolicella blend from Italy. You won't be disappointed."

Blake didn't know about that. He had a wine cellar at home and was pretty selective when it came to his vintages. But for some reason, none of that was very important right now.

When the waiter returned, he uncorked the bottle, then poured a bit into Blake's glass for him to approve. It was surprisingly good, and he wasn't the least bit dissatisfied.

After filling both glasses to the proper level, the waiter asked, "Have you made a dinner decision yet?"

Shannon ordered a bowl of stracciatella soup and a side of penne pasta with marinara sauce. Blake chose the spaghetti and meatballs, as well as a Caesar salad.

When the waiter returned to the kitchen, leaving them alone, Blake lifted his wineglass in a toast. "To the Rocking Chair Ranch."

Shannon smiled. "I'll drink to that."

They clinked their glasses, then took a drink.

"Mmm," Shannon said. "This is really nice."

She was right, but it wasn't just the wine that was nice. It was the evening spent with her.

"I heard that the ranch might be having some financial difficulties," he said.

Shannon seemed to weigh her response, then said, "That's true, although your uncle hopes to turn things around. It was in bad shape when Chloe inherited it, so the cattle operation needs to be built up. On top of that, some of the retired cowboys have limited incomes, but we didn't want to turn anyone away."

When Blake first arrived, he had a different opinion about the ranch, but now that he'd spent some time on the place and had gotten to know the people who lived and worked there, his views had changed.

"Is there anything I can do to help?" he asked.

"Thanks for the offer. If something comes up, I'll let you know. But we should be okay, especially if the rodeo sponsorship comes through."

"I'd heard about that. Do you have any idea how soon you'll know for sure?"

"Within a few days to a week. At least, that's what Nate thinks. He and Rex are the ones with the biggest connections."

Blake lifted his glass of wine and took a sip. "I hope it works out. It's a great idea, and one that's fitting— cowboys helping each other out."

Shannon smiled, her eyes glimmering in the candlelight. "Rex calls it the Rocking Chair Rodeo."

"I like the sound of that." Before Blake could offer any other thoughts, the waiter returned with their soup and salad.

After thanking the man, they both focused on their meal. It only took one bite to realize Papa Giovanni's food was every bit as good as the flower vendor said it would be.

"My soup is delicious," Shannon said. "And the bread is to die for."

"I heard that they're known for their pizza. Maybe, one of these days, we ought to order some for the guys at the ranch." Of course, if Blake was going to pull that off, he'd have to do it quickly, like tomorrow.

"I'm sure they'd enjoy a treat like that. It would also give Joy an evening off."

Blake lifted his glass. "Does she ever get a break?"

"So far, she hasn't wanted one. She loves cooking for an appreciative crowd. But I'm sure Sam would like to take her out on the town some night." Shannon shot a questioning gaze across the table, as if she expected Blake to have some kind of negative reaction to the comment.

"You know," he said, "I'm not concerned about my uncle dating anymore. I've seen how much better he's doing, and I now realize Joy is a big reason for that. Another is that he feels needed again, especially working on a ranch."

Shannon reached for the stem of her glass and fingered it. "I agree with you. Joy's put a smile in his heart. But there's also something to be said about living on the Rocking C, which is a familiar and comfortable setting for all the residents."

"I agree. The past few days have brought back a lot of good memories for me."

"You mean the summers when you stayed on Sam's ranch?"

"Yes. I'm sorry I didn't buy it from him when I had the chance. But I guess that's just as well. Still, there's something special about being on a ranch again."

"I felt the same way when I came here." She lifted her glass and took a sip. "I guess, in some ways, we have a lot in common."

Blake wasn't so sure that was true, but the thought interested him. "In what ways?"

"We both either lived or spent time on ranches as kids, and we both lost a parent."

That *was* true, but in Shannon's case, both her father and mother had died. Of course, she'd been an adult when her dad passed. And Blake still had his mom, although they weren't particularly close. He suspected that was because he resembled his father so much—at least, in appearance.

Even as a young child, he'd known his parents hadn't been happy. He'd also suspected that he reminded his mom of his dad and the mistake she'd made in marrying him. That was one reason he'd tried so hard to make her and his grandparents proud of the man he'd become.

"How old were you when you lost your dad?" she asked.

"I was six. While he was snow-skiing, he hit a patch of ice and crashed into a tree. He died instantly."

"Where were you when it happened?"

"At home with the nanny. He and my mom had gone to Vail with my grandparents."

"I guess it's probably good that you weren't with them."

Blake shrugged. "My parents and grandparents used to vacation together, but they didn't include me very often." In fact, they'd only lived an hour or so from Disneyland, and his first visit had been with a friend from school.

"So you didn't have any big family vacations?"

"Only when we visited Sam and Nellie." His

thoughts drifted to the loss that had nearly unraveled him as a kid, the one he'd thought he'd put way behind him. "The sad thing is, I hardly remember my dad anymore. Most of my memories are just the things Sam and Nellie told me about him, things he'd said or done long before I was born."

"I'm sorry," she said. "I was fortunate because my dad kept a lot of pictures of my mom around. In fact, I don't think he got rid of any of her belongings. If I hadn't known any better, I would have thought that she still lived with us."

On the other hand, Blake's mom had cleaned out his father's side of the closet before the funeral, which was one reason he'd taken it so hard. It was as if the man had completely disappeared from their lives without a trace.

"I guess you could say that I was fortunate, too." Blake offered her a wry grin. "My grandfather paid for me to see the best therapist in LA."

Granddad had also purchased him a new bike, as well as a PlayStation, which he'd hoped would take Blake's mind off his grief.

All of that had helped, he supposed, but it would have been nice to have had someone in his mother's family to talk to. Sam and Nellie were always available, but he hadn't been allowed to travel to Texas to visit them until he was twelve.

When the waiter returned for their empty plates, he left a dessert menu and mentioned that the tiramisu was a customer favorite.

Before either of them could look over their other options, a boom of thunder sounded outside, followed

closely by a flash of lightning that lit up their cozy
corner booth.

Shannon glanced out the rain-splattered window
then set the dessert menu aside. "Maybe we ought
to return to the house. If you want something sweet,
there's ice cream in the freezer and probably plenty
of leftover chocolate chip cookies."

Blake wasn't a big dessert eater, unless it was a
special occasion, which this evening seemed to be.
But Shannon was already reaching for her purse and
was clearly ready to go.

"Is that thunder bothering you?" he asked. "Or
are you just worried about the weather?"

"The rain we've had over the past couple of days
was only part of a series of storms on their way in
from the gulf. And when we drove here, I noticed
that the creek had already risen pretty high."

Blake signaled for the waiter, then asked for the
bill. After paying with cash and leaving a generous
tip, he stood and waited for Shannon to slide from
the booth. Then he followed her out of the restaurant.

Once they were standing outside under the awning, the rain was now coming down at a steady
clip. So he said "Let's hurry to the car to avoid getting soaked."

Melissa would have balked at an idea like that
and insisted he leave her under the awning so she
wouldn't get her hair wet or ruin her makeup.

On the other hand, Shannon, who'd been fidgety just moments ago, appeared to be delighted at
the suggestion. "I *love* the rain. When I was a kid,

I used to slip outside and play in it whenever I got the chance—or thought I could get away with it."

"No kidding? I wish I'd known you back then." It had been an odd thing for Blake to say, let alone think, but it was true. Shannon was an enigma, and he could only imagine the little girl she'd once been.

They made a mad dash to the car. As he opened the passenger door for her, she paused in the drizzling rain for a moment, then turned to him and smiled. "For what it's worth, I would have liked knowing you back then, too—during the summers when you visited Sam's ranch."

And obviously not when he'd been living in California, hobnobbing it with the rich and famous. He supposed that shouldn't come as any surprise. Shannon had been a country girl—and still was.

As the raindrops continued to fall, dancing on the strands of her hair and dampening her curls, she continued to stand outside the car. In spite of the chill in the air, she studied him as carefully as he studied her.

She had to look up to meet his gaze, water droplets clinging to her lashes. When she licked at her lips with the tip of her tongue, he did something stupid. Or maybe it was the smartest move he'd ever made.

He bent his head and kissed her, slowly at first, tenderly. Then, as her arms slipped around his neck, as she pulled him closer, his desire for her spun out of control.

He lost himself in her touch, in her taste. And it didn't seem to matter one little bit that they were getting soaked to the gills.

A burst of thunder roared, and the lightning

flashed again. But Blake ignored the weather and focused on the series of fireworks going off in his head.

No doubt his and Shannon's chemistry would lead to unspeakable passion—if he dared let it.

Shannon had no idea how long she and Blake would have stood outside in the rain, necking like a couple of kids with no responsibilities, no reason to give their actions any thought. If she hadn't finally decided to put an end to it, she might have kissed him until... Well, until one of them suggested they go someplace warm and dry, where they could finish what they'd started.

As she drew her lips from his, she wasn't sure what to say, so she opted to smile and make light of whatever was burning between them. "There's nothing like getting heated up and taking a cold shower at the same time."

Blake didn't return her smile. Instead, he placed a hand on her jaw and studied her intently. The blood-stirring arousal in his gaze was just as obvious as it had been in his kiss.

"For the record," he said, "that kind of crazy, spontaneous kiss was a first for me."

At his revelation, her pulse spiked and her heart raced. Kissing in the rain with such wild and reckless abandon had been a first for her, too. And now that she'd experienced passion like that, she didn't want it to be the one and only time.

She wouldn't admit it, though. Especially to a handsome attorney who could have any woman he wanted. But he lived in California, so his choice of lovers would be limited to that neck of the woods.

His thumb caressed her cheek, sending her thoughts tumbling into a senseless hodgepodge. Then, with a sigh, he released her. "We'd better get out of here."

Shannon nodded her agreement. After slipping into the passenger seat and closing the door, she fingered her lips, still puffed and tingly from the sweet, sensual assault. But once Blake began to climb into the car, before he got behind the wheel, she dropped her hand into her lap so he wouldn't know how deeply she'd been affected.

If Blake had any thoughts or reservations about what they'd done, he didn't mention it. In fact, as he started the engine, he didn't say anything at all. And neither did Shannon.

They drove in silence, but that mind-spinning kiss seemed to have taken on a life of its own, becoming an invisible passenger that sat between them, clamoring for attention.

At least, the thought of it was banging and clanging around in her brain like the little steel ball in a pinball machine.

Kissing Blake had felt so right, yet at the same time, it seemed wrong. He'd be flying back to Los Angeles soon, and where would that leave them?

Where would that leave *her*?

Her life would go back to usual, she supposed. Still, something had permanently changed, and she knew that, in some ways, she'd never be the same again.

"I'll get the heater going," Blake said, a boyish grin tugging at his lips. "Sam and the others would never forgive me if I let the head nurse catch pneumonia."

So he was downplaying it, too. Then again, it was only natural that he'd focus on their physical comfort, since they were both damp and cold. But in doing so, he'd bypassed the "now what?" question altogether.

There really was no reason to bring it up, though. Why even broach the subject when there was no logical answer?

As the warm air began to flow into the car, Shannon thanked him for dinner.

"My pleasure," he said.

They both let it go at that, and the silence continued for another mile or two.

Finally, Blake shot a glance her way. "Are you doing okay?"

"Yes, I'm fine." And she really was. She might be a little surprised and conflicted by it all, but she was definitely okay. In fact, even wet and chilled to the bone, she'd never felt so alive.

Who would have guessed that Blake's kiss could make her feel this way?

Clearly, he wasn't the right man for her, so nothing could ever become of the passionate moment they'd shared in the drizzling rain tonight.

As she tried to convince herself of that fact, her argument fell flat, and she realized she was wrong. Something certainly *was* going to come of it. The memory alone was going to last a long, long time.

Sure, she'd been kissed before, but never like that.

Her mind and her hormones were still swirling, and she wasn't sure what to do about it.

One thing was certain, though. Now that she'd experienced passion and desire at their finest, she'd never settle for less in a kiss.

Or less in a man.

Last night's rain had been a big one, no doubt closing the road. But the storm that had raged inside Blake had kept him tossing and turning all night.

He'd never been so tempted to revamp his plans for the sake of spending the night with a woman. But Nurse Shannon had knocked him completely off stride.

Not that he'd let his law firm down, close his practice and remain in Texas, but he couldn't just walk away from the Rocking C without …

Oh, hell. He wanted more time to get to know Shannon a little better. The woman hadn't just intrigued him, she seemed to have cast some kind of spell on him. Suffice it to say, he wasn't ready to leave just yet, so he'd have to get ahold of Carol.

Out of habit, he reached for his cell and dialed the office, but he couldn't get a signal. So he picked the landline in Sam's kitchenette and placed the call.

It was two hours earlier in California, which meant Carol hadn't gotten to work yet, but he left her a message and asked her to cancel his flight. He used the rain and flooding as an excuse, telling her that he couldn't make it to the Houston airport until the water receded. Which, technically, was true. But that wasn't the only reason. Even if the road was open, he was still reeling from that kiss he'd shared with Shannon.

He wrapped up his message by saying, "I'll let you know when you can reschedule my return."

Carol would assume that he was eager to get back to Los Angeles because of all the work piling up on his desk. But why wouldn't she? She knew how focused he was on his law practice, so it would never cross her mind that he might not be in any big hurry to leave the Rocking C, even if the creek hadn't risen.

After disconnecting the line, he headed to the barn, taking care to avoid the puddles and noting the mess last night's wind had left behind, the scattered leaves and twigs. Now that he would be staying on the ranch a little longer, he'd better make himself useful, and the best way to do that was to go in search of his uncle and find out what he could do to help out around the place.

When Blake was a kid, he knew to look for Sam in the barn first. And sure enough, that's exactly where he found him this morning, repairing one of the stable gates.

A big black mare with white fetlocks was tied to a post about five feet away. She snorted and appeared fidgety. Clearly, she wasn't too happy about being temporarily displaced.

"What's going on?" Blake asked.

Sam looked up from his work. "Lady Luck over there went ballistic during the thunderstorm and kicked her stall apart last night."

"Need a hand?"

Sam's brow furrowed. "I can use all the help I can

get around here, but the hands are fixing a downed fence along Greenly Road. And Nate's looking for lost cattle."

Blake slipped his fingers into the front pockets of his jeans. "I'm available."

Sam looked at him as if he'd fallen off a skittish horse and conked his head.

Blake bit back a laugh. "I might not have done this kind of work in years, but I had a good teacher, and I still remember my training. You know what they say. It's just like riding a bike."

When Sam realized Blake was serious, he chuckled. "I wish it were that easy. But I gotta tell you, some of the hands I hired would be better off working at a bicycle shop in town."

"Are they that green?"

"They're coming along—*finally*. But I'm not sure you can teach a man how to be a good cowboy. It's not just a matter of wearing a Stetson and a Western shirt or knowing how to saddle a horse. As far as I'm concerned, it's a gift."

Sam might be right about that, although Blake suspected growing up on a ranch made a big difference.

"Your dad had a real knack for working cattle," Sam added. "But he gave it all up when he married your mom. And believe it or not, I once thought you had it, too." Sam returned his focus to the gate, then nodded at a pile of lumber. "Would you bring a slat of wood over here?"

"Sure."

Moments later, Blake was working alongside Sam,

just like he'd done that last summer he'd spent on his uncle's ranch. Before long, all the training and instruction came back to him.

"It's too bad you weren't able to hire more experienced hands," he told his uncle.

"Well, I couldn't afford to. Things will be different someday, but the money just isn't there yet."

"Is the ranch financially stable?"

Sam sighed. "It is for the time being, but there were back taxes owed and repairs that needed to be made. Hell, the barn was falling apart, so that was the first thing I had to get fixed."

So that was the reason for the fresh coat of red paint. It hadn't been a matter of making the place look good.

"Just so you know," Sam added, "I offered a substantial loan to Chloe and Joe so they could make other improvements, buy more cattle and hire more experienced hands, but they turned me down. They want the Rocking C to be self-supportive, and I have to agree."

Blake hadn't met the couple, but he liked their way of thinking.

"Chloe and Joe are more worried about having to turn away a retired cowboy who needs a place to live out his final days."

Maybe Blake could help with that. "I've got some money I can spare, and my CPA is always suggesting that I fund a charity. I could write a check to the Rocking Chair Ranch."

"Chloe and Joe would rather not resort to fundraising—at least, not yet. They're worried about people wanting to come in and try to change the vision they have for the ranch."

Blake pondered that reasoning for a moment, not sure that he agreed. They couldn't very well help any of those men if they had to shut down and close the doors.

"I'll tell you what," Blake said. "I'll write a generous check to pay for my keep this past week. Besides, that'll also show Joy and Shannon that I have a good side. And believe it or not, I *do* have one."

"I know you do. Nellie and I saw clear signs of it whenever you'd come to visit. But be careful. Your grandfather's way of showing his love or fixing problems was to shower his family with gifts, just like that fancy video game set he gave you after your father died. I couldn't see the sense in that. Wouldn't a fishing trip or a game of catch in the evenings have worked better for a kid missing his daddy?"

"Probably."

Sam let out a *humph*. "Sometimes a man has to address his feelings and not avoid them, no matter how uncomfortable that might make him. If you'd been living with Nellie and me when your father died, I wouldn't have tried to distract you from your grief. I would have let you talk about it whenever you needed to."

"I talked about it." He'd also talked about the fact that neither his mother nor his grandparents seemed to be especially torn up by the loss of his father.

Sam probably wouldn't think a high-dollar therapist was the answer, especially since Dr. Boroughs had merely given Blake's mom and her family a way to pass the buck and not have to deal with a broken-hearted kid.

Still, it was not as though Granddad hadn't been loving or supportive. He just hadn't been one to talk about feelings.

On the other hand, Sam rarely kept his thoughts or emotions secret, which was just further evidence that the two men had been cut from different bolts of cloth. So for that reason, Blake was about to let the topic drop and get back to work when an idea struck, one he never would have considered when he first arrived. "Did you ever think about using the retired cowboys to mentor the younger hands?"

"I could," Sam said, "but Rex and the other guys tend to bitch and holler at them more often than not. And so I doubt anyone would listen to them."

"Maybe you should have a talk with the older cowboys and tell them how badly their wisdom and experience is needed. They might be easier on the hired men and less critical. I'd think that might make your job a whole lot easier. You certainly can't be everywhere at once."

Sam seemed to think on that a moment, then said, "That actually might work. The whole idea was to not only offer the retirees a familiar environment, but to make them feel useful."

"I can see the change that took place in you when you took this position. I also noticed a robust glow on Gerald McInerny, the guy who works in the garden."

"Good point. And boy do we appreciate his contributions to our meals." Sam didn't say any more, but Blake could tell he was seriously considering the idea while they worked.

After he and his uncle repaired the broken slats on the stall gate and reattached the hinges, Sam nodded toward the black mare. "Bring Lady Luck here so we can stable her again."

Blake did as instructed, but just as he was going to release the horse into the stall, thunder rumbled in the distance, and Lady Luck reared, then bucked and kicked.

"Steady, girl." Sam tried to calm her, but she wasn't convinced that he'd keep her safe from the threatening sound.

When another roar of thunder sounded through the barn, Lady Luck reared again, desperate to get away. In the process, her rear hoof struck Blake square in the knee and knocked him to the ground.

He swore under his breath, not only from the pain, but in frustration because Sam was left to calm the horse on his own. Moments later, Lady Luck had been stabled, although she was still fidgety.

"You okay?" Sam asked.

"I'll be fine."

Sam eased closer. "Can you walk?"

"Yeah." Maybe. Blake stroked his knee, which seemed a bit swollen already. "Just give me a minute or two."

"All right. Once you're on your feet, go into the house and let Shannon have a look at it."

"That's not necessary." At least, he hoped the injury wouldn't inconvenience him very long.

Sam clucked his tongue. "Don't pull a Nate on me."

"What do you mean?"

"He doesn't like to seek medical attention."

"I thought that was because he wanted you and everyone else to think he was tough."

"Partly, but I suspect there's a little more to it than that." Sam reached out his hand, and Blake took it.

With his uncle's help, he was able to stand up, but he couldn't put his full weight on his right leg.

"Slip your arm around me," Sam said. "I'll help you into the house."

Blake complied, but he wasn't happy about it. He never liked to show any sign of weakness or to allow anyone to see his vulnerability. He supposed it wouldn't be so bad if that person was a medical professional, but he'd prefer to face Doc Nelson and admit that he'd been a little careless and had gotten on the wrong side of a frightened horse.

But Shannon? Blake didn't blame Nate for risking infection and hiding from the pretty nurse in the barn after he got cut on that beer bottle.

When Blake faced Shannon, he wanted to do so standing tall and whole, a man at his finest.

Still, even though he found himself leaning on his uncle and hobbling into the house, it wasn't just his physical appearance or virility he wanted Shannon to admire. It was the man inside, the man Melissa had failed to see, let alone value.

Chapter Nine

Shannon had just hung up the phone after talking to Doc Nelson when Sam and Blake entered the office. Blake's brow was creased as he leaned against his uncle and limped into the room.

"What happened?" She closed the patient file in which she'd just made a notation and rose from her desk.

Sam looked at Blake, apparently waiting for the younger man to answer. When he didn't, Sam spoke for him. "Blake had a run-in with Lady Luck and lost."

She gazed at the California attorney in disbelief. "You were *gambling*?"

"With my life, it seems." Blake's grimace morphed into a wry grin, albeit one that appeared to be forced.

"Apparently I've been away from the ranch life so long that I reverted back to my greenhorn days. A mare kicked, and I didn't get out of the way soon enough. She got me in the knee. But it's not serious. It's just a little bruised and sore."

"A greenhorn, huh?" She couldn't help but smile. "You sound like most of the seasoned cowboys around here. None of them want me to know when they're sick or hurting."

Sam led Blake near the chairs that lined a wall, although neither of them took a seat.

"Now that you're in good hands," Sam said, "I'm going back to the barn."

Shannon might be competent and able to handle most of the injuries that occurred on the ranch, but for the first time in her short career, she felt a little unbalanced by a patient. And when Sam left, closing the door behind him, the walls seemed to close in on her, on *them*.

"You know," Blake said, "this really isn't necessary."

"Sam thinks it is. And so do I." She glanced at his dusty denim jeans, which hid his injured knee.

She moved close to Blake, close enough to examine him. Close enough to catch a hint of his musky, leather-laced scent. But she shook off her attraction and assumed her best professional stance.

"I'm afraid you're going to have to remove your pants," she said, "Otherwise, I'll have to cut them."

She expected him to object, to insist again that there was no need for her to examine his knee. Instead, she watched a crooked, playful grin stretch across his face.

While he unbuckled his belt, his eyes never left hers. He continued to watch her, to unravel her, as he unbuttoned his waistband.

Then he reached for the zipper. *Zzziiip.*

Her feminine senses sharpened and desire soared. This was *so* not what she'd expected when she'd told him to remove his pants.

As he peeled off his jeans, his gaze remained locked on hers. She was both tempted to watch the unveiling and afraid to look at the same time. What if she made a giddy, breathless fool out of herself, like a drunken bridesmaid at a wild bachelorette party?

Oh, for Pete's sake. This was no big deal. Lots of men had stripped down in front of her before, oodles of them. All but Michael had been for medical reasons. Still, this particular undressing threatened to be her undoing.

Heck, she felt almost…virginal. And while she'd had sex before, she really didn't consider herself to be all that experienced.

His pants slid over his hips, revealing a pair of black boxer briefs that fit him perfectly, like those a sexy male model flashed in a magazine advertisement.

She tried to think of an excuse to either look away or to watch him drop his drawers further, but she couldn't seem to do either.

When he swayed on his feet, no doubt because of his injury, her nursing instincts finally kicked into high gear.

"Here," she said, reaching out to steady him.

His arm, strong and muscular, slid around her, setting off a jingle-jangle of emotions that had very little to do with his safety or her usual attempt to offer a little TLC to a patient.

"Maybe you better help me back into a chair," he said. "My knee isn't as painful as it'll be if I try to step out of these pants."

Once he took a seat, she knelt beside him so she could get a good look at his swollen knee, which bore a dark, nasty bruise. No wonder he was limping. It had to hurt like hell, although she didn't think it was broken. Still, an X-ray was probably in order. And that meant he'd have to go to the Brighton Valley Medical Center, something she thought he might object to.

She fingered the tender area carefully. Even though she was further convinced that the injury probably wasn't serious, she was reluctant to end the exam.

Or, to be more truthful, she was reluctant to stop touching him.

She reminded herself that she was just doing her job and wanted to be thorough. But if that were the case, why were her fingers trembling, her heart pounding and her blood rushing to her feminine parts?

Like it or not, it took all she could muster to remove her hands and keep them to herself.

For a guy who'd been reluctant to enter Shannon's office with a bum leg, Blake wasn't so eager to skedaddle now. Not after being on the receiving end of her gentle fingers, her soft breath, the worried look upon her face.

In fact, he had a feeling she was doing more than examining his knee, especially since he was sitting here with his pants dropped down to his ankles.

Just seeing her kneeling at his feet, her hair a tumble of curls a man could get his fingers tangled up in, her citrusy scent wafting around him, was enough to relieve his pain altogether. In fact, he was sorely tempted to do something completely out of line. Did he have the nerve to reach down, to cup her jaw and draw her face up to his for another kiss?

Yes, but he'd better not risk it. The two of them didn't have a chance in hell of striking up anything other than a one-night fling. And something told him Shannon wouldn't agree to something like that.

Interestingly enough, making a commitment of any kind to her had been out of the question when they'd first met. But now that he knew her better, now that she'd kissed him senseless, he might be willing to reconsider.

But that was crazy. They lived halfway across the country from each other, so he'd better not even suggest it. Besides, he could hardly walk right now, and if he and Shannon ever made love, he wanted to be completely mobile and at the top of his game.

So rather than act upon his impulse, he tamped it down and focused on the reason he was here.

"So what's your diagnosis?" he asked.

She withdrew her fingers from his skin, leaving

it warm and still buzzing from her touch. When she gazed up at him, she flushed.

Was she embarrassed about the odd predicament they'd found themselves in? He certainly wasn't, although he could easily become sexually frustrated.

She slowly rose from the floor and placed her hands on her hips. "You should probably stay off your feet for a while. I'm sure it hurts, so I can give you some ibuprofen."

"That's okay." He wanted her to know he was tough, that he could suck up the pain. "It feels a lot better now."

He bent forward, reached for the waistband of his jeans and pulled them up past his knees. Then he stood upright and tried to finish the job without putting his full weight on that right leg. But he struggled to keep his balance.

"Would you like me to help?" she asked.

Seriously? He shot her a wry grin. "If I was trying to take them off completely, I'd love to have your help."

It had been a joke—well, kind of. But clearly, the truth of it struck them both, stirring up thoughts he shouldn't allow himself to have. Thoughts he'd been having already.

He'd also kissed her before. And the door to her office was closed. Who was going to be the wiser?

Before he could consider the repercussions of what he was about to do, he removed his hands from his waistband, leaving it unbuttoned, and cupped her cheeks.

Her eyes widened in surprise, but she didn't back away, which was all the invitation he needed.

As their mouths met, her lips parted, allowing his tongue to seek hers, to tip and to taste, to tempt and to taunt.

She placed her hands on his waist, her fingers grazing his skin and lighting him on fire.

He slipped his arms around her, pulling her close, stroking her back, exploring the gentle curves that lay behind her baggy scrubs. The kiss deepened, intensifying to one that damn near screamed their mutual need.

But then what?

Shannon was on duty, and he wasn't anywhere near 100 percent. So he slowly drew away, breaking the kiss and ending the spell she'd cast on him.

For lack of any other reasonable explanation or excuse, he said, "I'd better get out of here and let you go back to work."

Then he left her gaping at him, probably pondering the same thing he was now wondering.

What in the hell were they going to do with the growing desire to be more than friends?

Hours after Blake had walked—or rather hobbled— out of Shannon's office, she continued to relive that last kiss, to ponder what it had meant and why it continued to happen.

He'd never broached the idea of dating—or anything else for that matter. He'd be leaving soon, so maybe that's why. But wouldn't most men press for something more, even if they weren't free to make a commitment?

Not that she'd agree to a one-time thing.

Or would she? Michael had been her one and only lover, and she'd thought their sexual relationship had been okay, but Michael's kisses had never affected her the way Blake's did.

At the time, she'd suspected that there'd been something missing, but she hadn't been exactly sure what it was. But she certainly knew what it was now.

What would she do if she never had the chance to feel that kind of heat, that kind of desire again?

Oh, for Pete's sake. That was silly. There had to be other men who could make her weak in the knees.

For the rest of the day, her thoughts had continued to bounce around like that, making her feel as though she were plucking daisy petals. I want him, I want him not. And when evening rolled around, she wasn't any closer to having an answer.

By nine o'clock the residents had all gone to their rooms and turned in for the night. The sofa on which Shannon slept when she stayed at the ranch was located in a small room just off the office. So she could have gone inside, shut the door for privacy and tried to get some sleep. But since she still couldn't seem to get Blake off her mind, she'd probably toss and turn for hours.

After helping Darlene pass out the bedtime medication and make a final check on the residents, Shannon headed for the kitchen to fix herself a snack and a cup of cocoa. There was probably some pie leftover. If so, she'd take it into the living room and turn on the television, setting the volume to low.

When she reached the main part of the house, she

realized she wasn't the only one still awake. Blake had beaten her to the TV and claimed a prime spot on the sofa. He'd yet to notice her, so she probably should have left him there and retired for the night. Only trouble was, now that she'd seen him, she was even more wide awake than ever.

Besides, shouldn't they talk about what was going on between them? They'd already shared three heated kisses. What did it mean?

Determined to get an answer, she made her way to where he sat.

Upon hearing her footsteps, he glanced up and grinned. "Hey, are you up for a movie? It's a Western—and a good one."

"Maybe." She returned his smile. "I'm going to fix a cup of hot cocoa. Would you like me to make one for you, too?"

"Sure, that would be great."

Since everyone else had turned in for the night—other than Darlene, who was probably doing her homework for an online college class she was taking—they'd have an opportunity to talk during the commercial breaks.

When he'd left her office earlier today, after the kiss he'd instigated, he'd acted as though it hadn't affected him at all. But if it hadn't, then why had he done it?

And why had she let him?

Because she was seriously attracted to the man, drawn to him like a frisky kitten to catnip, that's why. But there was so much more to a relationship than hot kisses, strong chemistry and raging hormones.

She'd always thought she'd marry a man like her father, a man she'd once thought wouldn't be easy to find in a town like Brighton Valley. But now that she'd kissed Blake, she realized her dream lover would not only have to be kind and gentle, but he'd also need to set her body on fire. And that could make her Mr. Right nearly impossible to find.

But what was wrong with wanting a man who could not only touch her heart and calm her nerves, but who could also spark a flame in her soul? Was that too much to ask?

Ten minutes later, Shannon returned to the living room carrying a tray holding mugs of hot cocoa, as well as two small plates, each one bearing a slice of the chocolate-mint pie Joy had made for tonight's dessert.

"Service with a smile," she said, as she placed the goodies on the coffee table. Then she handed a cup to Blake.

He thanked her and patted the cushion beside him, so she took a seat.

"What are you watching?" she asked.

"It's an old John Wayne movie called *The Cowboys*. I've seen it before. It's about a rancher who has to take his cattle to market, but is abandoned by his ranch hands. So he hires a bunch of kids to help."

Shannon blew across the rim of her mug and watched the steam rise. Then she took a sip. "Does it remind you of Sam taking on the young hands at the Rocking C?"

"I guess so. I was actually remembering what it

was like to ride with him and the cowboys on his ranch." A slow smile spread across his face.

"Sounds like you have some good memories," she said.

"A lot of them. During the school year, I lived in the city, which had plenty of perks. But when summer came along, I'd get to ride and rope from sunup to sundown."

"So you worked while on vacation?"

"It didn't seem like it. I might have had a lot of chores to do, but on weekends, Sam and I would go fishing or down to the ball fields. Looking back, I had the best of both worlds."

It sounded like he had. "Do you miss the city?"

"The funny thing is, when I'm there, I'm happy with that life. But when I'm here, I don't have the urge to rush back to it. I guess that's because I don't miss the smog, the traffic or fast pace."

Did that mean he was tempted to stay in Texas? Or even willing to come back to the ranch and visit more often? Sam would certainly like it if he did. And so would Shannon, especially if it allowed them to cultivate their budding friendship, if that was what you could even call it.

He must miss his work and his friends, though. Maybe even a lover. A man as gorgeous and successful as Blake must have at least one lady in the wings. Shoot, he probably had his choice of dozens. But she couldn't very well ask, could she?

"I'm a little surprised you're still here," she said, prompting the discussion she wanted to have.

"Actually, so am I." He paused a beat, and when

she glanced his way, a crease in his brow suggested that he might be worried that he'd revealed too much.

She realized she was reading too much into his expression when he shrugged and added, "I'm going to leave once the water recedes."

So dragging out his stay had nothing to do with kissing her.

As much as she'd like to bemoan that fact, she couldn't very well let it get to her. He wasn't long for the Rocking C, so what did it matter if he had another woman back in California, eager for him to get home?

Shannon took another sip of cocoa and slumped back in her seat. Blake was completely wrong for her anyway—no matter which way she tried to spin it.

As Blake sat beside Shannon, close enough to reach out and take her hand in his, he lost interest in the movie.

Only a fool would try to convince himself that he hadn't been thinking about her all day and insisting that their kisses hadn't meant a thing. In fact, he was tempted to take her in his arms again, to kiss her senseless, then invite her back to the small house in which he was staying, where they could make love until dawn.

But that was crazy.

Wasn't it?

He had nothing to offer her other than a night or two of pleasure, then he'd be gone. Would she be content with that?

Something told him she wouldn't be. Another man might have ditched the erotic thoughts he'd been having and focus on the movie. But Blake couldn't seem to get his mind off those fiery kisses and the sexy nurse seated beside him.

"How's that leg?" she asked.

It still hurt, but he could put more weight on it now. Yet rather than giving her an honest answer, he couldn't help but toss her a flirtatious grin. "Do you want me to drop my pants again so you can take a look?"

Her cheeks flushed. "That's probably not necessary."

No, not for any medical reason. But he could see the wheels turning in her mind, no doubt going over those blasted questions he'd been asking himself, ever since that last kiss. And he sensed the yearning in her eyes, the desire.

He had a feeling they'd be in agreement about taking a little walk to Sam's place, which was empty and waiting for someone to enjoy the pleasures of that double bed.

"What are we going to do about this?" he finally asked, opening the door to discussion and the suggestion of a tumble in the hay.

"About what?" she asked.

"This," said Blake, gesturing between them. "You know what I mean. There's something going on here, between us. Ever since we kissed."

Shannon blushed. "I know what I'd like to do," she said. "But you'll be leaving soon. Right?"

He'd like to stretch out his visit, but as it was, he'd already been away from the office way too long. "I'm going to fly out in a day or so, as soon as the road opens and I can drive to Houston."

She bit down on her bottom lip, a pensive reaction

that sent his blood racing. He suspected she was about to agree to the suggestion he hadn't actually spelled out.

That is, until she looked up, caught his eye and said, "Believe it or not, I'm an old-fashioned girl."

Which meant what? That before making love she wanted a ring, a white lace gown, a walk down the aisle to the altar and a vow that they would last forever?

He supposed he couldn't blame her for that. And in a way, he actually admired her for it. But that wasn't something he could offer her.

They sat quietly for a while, but her words still hung in the air. And so did his desire for her.

He reached for her hand, feeling its warmth, its strength, its fragility. "I'm afraid that, under the circumstances, I can't give you any kind of commitment. But I can give you tonight—and a promise to make it worth your time."

"I have no doubt about that. I've kissed you enough to know how good making love would be."

That's exactly why he'd broached the subject. He knew that things would be even better than good. He knew it in his heart, in his soul.

But he couldn't very well sit beside her the rest of the evening, battling a powerful arousal that rose up each time he thought about their fiery kisses.

"I'd better turn in for the night," he said, slowly getting to his feet. "If you have any second thoughts, you know where to find me."

Then he headed back to Sam's place alone, wishing he could have offered her more than what would only amount to a one-night stand. But he'd established a lucrative career for himself in LA that was a far cry from the bucolic life in Brighton Valley. So it was best for everyone involved if he kept his focus.

Still, while his head was convinced, there were a few other parts of him that insisted he should have put up a better argument.

As much as Blake would like to hang out on the Rocking C for an indefinite period of time and wait for Shannon to have a change of heart, he really had to get back to the office—and for more reasons than his work ethic.

The attraction brewing between him and the head nurse was sure to boil over into a heated mess if he wasn't careful.

He wasn't sure if she was struggling with their obvious attraction as badly as he was, but if she'd had any second thoughts about joining him at Sam's place last night, they certainly hadn't convinced her to do it.

On the upside, the rain had stopped several hours before dawn, and at breakfast, one of the young hands had said the road was open again, at least temporarily. So the excuse Blake had given Carol about staying in Texas was no longer valid. Just moments ago, he'd called her and told her to go ahead and schedule his return flight because, by the look of those dark incoming clouds, the road wasn't going to stay open for long.

All he had left to do, besides telling Shannon goodbye, was to let his uncle know that he was leaving. So he crossed the yard in search of Sam. He didn't have to go far. Sam was just walking out of the big house, holding Joy's hand. She was carrying her purse.

"Where are you two going?" Blake asked.

"Into town for ranch supplies and groceries," Sam said. "While we're gone, my girl and I are going to have lunch and see a movie."

"Going on a date, huh?" Blake couldn't help but smile. He might have had doubts about Joy in the past, but he'd come to realize that she was a good-hearted woman. "You both deserve some time away from the ranch."

"I think so, too." Sam slipped an arm around his "girl" and grinned. "But you don't need to worry about anyone dropping the ball. Joy already prepared sandwiches and potato salad for the rest of you to eat. Shannon said she'd take over the kitchen duties today, and I'm leaving Nate Gallagher in charge of the ranch."

"Sounds like you have it all covered."

"I wouldn't have been able to talk Joy into leaving if I hadn't planned it out. But give us a call if you need us. Our cell phones should work once we get beyond the Rio Rico Bridge."

"Will do," Blake said. "And have fun. But just so you know, I might not be here when you return. I need to get back to LA."

His uncle gave him a once over, no doubt checking out his jeans and boots. "So you're done playing cowboy?"

"For the time being." It was funny, though. After falling back into the swing of ranch life, however briefly, he was going to miss it when he returned home.

Sam glanced down at Blake's knee. "I see you're up and about, so I take it you're on the mend."

"Yep. I can even walk on it without hobbling too badly."

"Good." Sam stroked Joy's back, then nodded toward the area near the barn, where the vehicles were parked. "Let's go, honey. We have a lot to do and need to get back before the rain hits again."

The couple walked away, hand in hand. Blake watched them go until they reached the ranch pickup they'd be driving into town.

Sam was clearly happy these days and looking better and healthier than he had in well over a year. And Joy appeared to really care for him.

So Blake's time in Texas had been well spent. At least as far as his uncle was concerned.

He wished he could say the same thing about the week he'd spent getting to know Shannon. Not that he hadn't enjoyed it, but he'd be spinning his wheels if he hung around her any longer. He wasn't sure what he was feeling for her—beyond desire—or what, if anything, he could do about it.

Maybe, after he returned to California, the puzzle pieces would fall into place. He sure hoped so because, crazy as it might sound, he was finding ranch life a little too appealing, especially after he'd made a wise and solid decision about the direction his life needed to take.

Back when he'd been studying for the bar, Sam had tried to talk him into giving it all up—the city, the dream of a high-dollar career. Blake had refused to consider it then, and there was far more holding him in California now.

As the screen door squeaked open, he turned toward the house and watched Shannon walk out onto the porch. Admittedly, striking up a relationship with her might provide him with a bigger dilemma.

No, that wasn't true. She had dreams to work at the Brighton Valley Medical Center. And he'd created a good life for himself in Beverly Hills. He certainly wasn't going to leave it all behind and move to Texas.

Still, as Shannon made her way toward him, he realized he wanted more from her than the kisses they'd already shared. But just what would he be willing to give up for that chance?

He couldn't very well make a commitment to a woman who lived halfway across the country. Or could he?

"Now that the road is open," she said, "Alicia was able to come to work and relieve me. So, while I have the chance, I'm going to go home to check on things there."

"All right. I'm going to drive to Houston and catch a flight back to LA."

Her brow knit together ever so softly, as though she might be disappointed to see him go.

"I'll be back in a couple of weeks," he added.

Her expression softened into a smile. "Your uncle will be glad to hear that."

Yes, but was Shannon glad to hear it?

Before either of them could respond, the screen door squeaked open again. They both glanced toward the house to see one of the oldsters, his eyes wide, his voice frantic. "Shannon, come quick. Rex is having a heart attack."

Chapter Ten

Shannon's heart sprang to her throat as she rushed to the front door. She would have been quick to respond, even if the patient in question hadn't been one of her favorites.

"Where is he?" she asked Pete Hawkins, the elderly cowboy who'd called her to help.

"In his room. Alicia's with him, but after she called 9-1-1, she asked me to come and get you."

In spite of the promise Shannon had made Rex about doctors and hospitals, this was the one exception, the type of emergency she'd told him about. If Rex didn't get the medical treatment he needed, his physical condition could worsen, making him even more dependent than he already was.

Once Shannon reached the elderly cowboy's bedroom, she spotted him lying on the floor. Alicia was kneeling beside him, her stethoscope placed on his chest.

"Hey," Shannon said, trying to keep the worry from her voice. "What's going on in here?"

"It's nothing," Rex said.

She hoped he was right—and that he'd understand why the paramedics would be arriving with their lights flashing and siren blaring.

"Alicia is worried for nothing," Rex said, his face pale, his brow damp. "It was my own fault. I was trying to get to the john, and I jumped up too fast. The room began to swirl like a tilt-a-whirl at the county fair, and I just passed out. It's no big deal. Just a little vertigo. I get it all the time. So you may as well go home like you planned."

There was no way she'd leave the ranch now, no matter how competent Alicia might be.

"Passing out *is* a big deal," she told Rex. "And so is vertigo. Doc Nelson needs to know about it."

Rex swore under his breath. "Don't bother that old codger with something this minor. I told you I was fine."

"I think it's his heart." Alicia turned away from Rex and looked at Shannon, her gaze revealing her worry. "He's also been stroking his left arm."

"Aw, hell. That's only because I landed on my shoulder when I fell. It ain't my blasted heart. So call off the dogs, will you?" Rex glanced at the doorway, then blew out a sigh of relief. "Thank God. There's my lawyer now. Will you please tell these ladies to go about their business and leave me alone?"

Shannon turned toward the door, surprised to see Blake standing there. Somehow, in all the turmoil, she hadn't realized he'd followed her. His presence lent a comfort at a time like this. She'd have to thank him for not rushing off to the airport during all the excitement, something she'd thought he might do.

"Don't worry," Blake said, as he eased his way into the small bedroom. "I'll make sure your wishes are known. But I'm afraid I have to agree with the nurses. You should let Doc Nelson examine you. Then, at that time, you can choose your own treatment plan."

Alicia and Shannon continued to treat Rex for a possible heart attack. And he continued to object. Finally, a siren sounded in the distance, and within minutes, two paramedics entered the small room with a stretcher.

"Aw, crap," Rex said. "Who in the hell called them?"

"It doesn't matter," Shannon said. "Alicia and I have a responsibility to our patients and we're just following procedures."

Alicia provided her findings to the paramedics, then got to her feet and let them take over.

"We're going to take you to the medical center," the taller of the two paramedics told Rex.

"Like hell you will," the feisty old cowboy hollered.

At that, Shannon stroked Rex's arm. "Settle down. This is just a formality. I'm sure you'll be back before dinner." Then she turned to the medics. "He has a DNR on file. That's his biggest concern."

"No worries," the tall, lanky medic told Rex. "We'll make sure the hospital has your paperwork and honors your request."

"What's that paper called?" Rex asked Shannon. "The D…?"

"It's a DNR. It's part of your medical directive and will go with you." Then she spoke to the paramedics. "He doesn't want anyone to perform CPR on him or to hook him up on life support. He's ready to die and doesn't want any last-minute heroics."

"Don't worry," the shorter paramedic told Rex. "We've got your back."

At that assurance, Rex calmed down and allowed them to wheel him out to the ambulance.

"I'll be riding along with you," Alicia told Rex.

Shannon was tempted to go along, too, but someone needed to stay on the ranch. "Please keep me posted."

Alicia nodded, then followed the paramedics out, leaving Shannon and Blake alone in the room. As his gaze swept over her, her pulse soared. If she weren't careful, she might forget all about the emergency they'd just had.

Shake it off, she told herself. But she couldn't seem to.

Even though little alarms should be going off in her head, cautioning her not to make any false assumptions about what Blake might be thinking, what he might be feeling, she didn't get a single warning vibe.

Instead she was tempted to give him a hug for

sticking around and making Rex feel better about what the future might bring.

"You look like you could use some coffee," Blake said. "Why don't you join me for a cup in the kitchen?"

Apparently he wasn't in that big of a hurry to leave, and quite frankly, she was glad that he wasn't. "Sure, but I'll have to make it quick. I need to call Darlene and ask her to cover for me so I can go to the hospital. Having me there might help Rex go along with whatever treatment he needs."

"I'm sure you're right."

When he held out a hand in an after-you gesture, she headed down the hall, on her way to the kitchen. While concerned about Rex, she knew he was in good hands with Alicia.

Besides, this might be her last opportunity to spend some quality time with the man who was taking up more and more of her thoughts and showing up in her dreams.

Blake poured two mugs of coffee, then handed one to Shannon. As she added a splash of cream and a packet of sweetener, he nodded toward the front door. "Let's take this out onto the porch. It might be nice to get some fresh air while we can."

"All right." She followed him outside, then took a seat in one of the rockers.

He chose the one beside her. The sun, which had been shining when he woke up this morning, had disappeared behind a dark gray cloud. "Looks like we're going to get more rain."

"I know. If you want to get on the road, you probably shouldn't wait too long."

He knew that. But he hadn't even packed his bag yet, something he couldn't seem to get around to doing. And he wasn't about to ponder the reason. He knew that, too. Shannon had really gotten under his skin—but in the nicest way.

After taking a sip of coffee, he turned to the nurse he'd come to respect, the lovely woman who'd touched something deep inside of him. "I hope everyone at the Rocking C knows how lucky they are to have you. You're an amazing and dedicated nurse. I think you made a perfect career choice."

She seemed to glow a bit at his praise. "Thanks. I'm glad I was here today." She lifted her mug and took a drink. "Actually, I'd wanted to be a doctor, but that plan didn't work out."

Her admission surprised him. "Why not?"

"After my dad was diagnosed with cancer, the chemo made him so sick and weak that there was no way he could work. And I was so busy looking after him that I couldn't take on an extra job." Her shoulders slumped as she studied her mug without taking another sip. Then she looked at Blake. "My dad was a good man, but he hadn't put much away for a rainy day, so we lost the ranch."

"I'm sorry. That had to be a tough blow to not only lose your father, but your home, too."

"I'm just relieved that he never realized just how bad things had gotten. He'd loved that ranch, but especially liked the garage where he worked on old cars."

Blake made the natural assumption. "So you opted to go to nursing school instead."

"I'd thought about getting a student loan, but when Joy went through her divorce, she moved in with me. And... Well, considering the time I'd be spending, as well as the expense, nursing was the smartest and easiest route to take. It was certainly the cheapest one."

"*Our* Joy?" he asked, realizing the two had known each other before coming to work at the Rocking Chair Ranch.

"Yes. Joy was my dad's sister."

So the two women were related. He probably should have connected the dots, especially since Shannon had always defended Joy. But then again, why wouldn't she? Even Blake, who'd had so many doubts before, had come to realize that Joy was genuine, that she was warmhearted and kind.

Since Shannon was Joy's niece, she had to be the woman Sam had wanted to send to medical school. Yet for some reason that didn't bother him the way it would have if he'd realized that when he'd first arrived.

"Joy was twelve years older than my dad, and when their parents died, she practically raised him. So after her second husband left her both broke and homeless, she had nowhere else to go. That's when I insisted she stay with me."

"How'd she end up working here?"

"She needed a job, but she'd been a housewife for her entire life and didn't have any work experience. When I found out the ranch needed a cook and housekeeper, I realized she'd be perfect for the position. So

I pulled a few strings." Shannon glanced at Blake, tucked a strand of hair behind her ear and smiled. "It's worked out nicely for everyone involved."

He supposed she was right. The owners of the ranch, Chloe and Joe, not only had a good employee, but an amazing cook.

"Working here has given Joy a special purpose in life," Shannon added, "something she really never had. And now she has people to fuss over, to care for—folks who care for her, too. To top it all off, she fell in love with Sam."

Shannon was right about that, too. Now that Blake had gotten to know Joy better and seen the couple together, it was hard to deny their feelings were real. It was enough to make a man wonder if finding a loving, good-hearted woman wasn't just a fluke but a real possibility.

A car engine sounded in the distance, and Shannon got to her feet. "That must be Darlene. I need to go. I'd like to get back before those dark clouds roll in."

Blake admired Shannon's sense of responsibility, her concern for the residents. And like her, he needed to leave, too, but for some reason, he didn't. Instead, he reached for her mug and remained seated. "Give me a call and let me know how Rex is doing."

"I will." She studied him for a moment, as if trying to decide whether he was sincere. But he'd come to care about that old man, too.

She flashed him a smile, then strode off the porch and headed toward her car.

As he watched her go, he wondered if she might

be the kind of woman who'd love a man for who he really was—and not what he could provide her.

Sam said there were plenty of them out there, women who'd love a man unconditionally.

And I should know, Sam had said. *I've found two of them myself.*

Right now, Blake was willing to settle for one.

Three hours later, Blake stood on the porch, waiting for Shannon to return to the ranch.

Sam and Joy had come back just before sunset. Then Sam had gone in search of Nate. The cowboy who'd become Sam's right hand man had worked seven days straight, and Sam wanted him to go home while he still had a chance of getting across the bridge.

When a clap of thunder shook the ranch house, Blake began to pace the length of the wraparound porch in spite of a slight limp. He could have gone inside, where it was warm and dry, but he wasn't going to do that until he saw Shannon's car pull into the yard.

He wasn't even going to ponder his reason for wanting to know she'd made it back safely—or why he hadn't driven to Houston while he'd still had the chance.

A flash of lightning lit the sky, and the rain began to fall. Hopefully this would be the last in the series. The entire valley had been soaked and could stand to dry out.

Thank God they'd gotten Rex out of there before this new storm hit.

Shannon had called an hour earlier and told them that Rex was doing fine, although he was barking at the nursing staff and threatening to walk out if they gave him any trouble.

As it turned out, it hadn't been a heart attack after all. It was some kind of inner ear disorder, but Doc Nelson wanted to keep him at the hospital for a couple of days to run some tests. Shannon also said she planned to stop by her place to get a few things before returning to the Rocking C.

If Blake was ever going to get to the airport, he'd better do it now—before the rain hit. It was already beginning to sprinkle, and it wouldn't take much to fill the creek to overflowing again. But he wouldn't leave until Shannon was back, safe and sound.

That didn't mean his plans had changed. He still meant to fly home as soon as he could. But he'd be making return trips to Texas, now that he'd seen the place where Sam was living and working.

And now that he'd met Shannon.

Didn't he owe it to himself to see where his feelings for her might lead?

As the rain began to fall, he continued to walk the length of the porch and back again, ignoring the growing ache in his knee.

Where was she? He hoped she hadn't wasted too much time at her house.

When he heard the roar of an engine in the distance, he turned to search the length of the driveway, hoping Shannon had finally arrived. Instead, a black Ford Ranger with only a single windshield wiper working pulled into the yard and parked.

Blake didn't recognize the woman driving and wouldn't have given her much thought, but when she fumbled to reach the handle to the driver's door, he got a better view and realized something was wrong.

Her curly blond hair was a mess, and when her head drooped forward, resting on the steering wheel, he approached the small pickup. Water splattered her windows, but he could see inside. When she raised her head, he spotted bruises on her face, a cut over her left eye and a dribble of blood oozing from her nose.

It looked as though she'd been in a car accident, although the vehicle didn't have any notable damage.

He knocked lightly upon the driver's side window. She slowly turned and looked at him, but she appeared dazed. He suspected she'd been beaten and didn't wait for her to open the door.

"Ma'am?" he asked. "Are you all right?"

She swiped at the blood coming from her nose, leaving a smear on her upper lip. "Is Nate here?"

Blake had no idea what she wanted with the cowboy, but as he helped her out of the truck, he noticed something else about her—she had a good-sized baby bump.

Suspecting that her injuries weren't the result of an accident, he made a reasonable assumption. "Who did this to you?"

"Kenny. He…" She swayed and fingered her forehead. The other hand rested on her swollen womb. "Oh, God. I… Where's Nate?"

He didn't want to tell her that the man had gone home for the next day or two. She was in no condition to drive, should she decide to look for him. It was a wonder she'd made it to the Rocking C without running into a ditch—or worse.

She must have been desperate to get away from "Kenny." But why hadn't she gone to the police?

Before Blake could question her further, she slumped. He caught her before she collapsed to the ground. He had to get her out of the rain and into the house, so he started for the front door.

In spite of her obvious pregnancy, she was just a slip of a thing and couldn't weigh more than a hundred pounds.

"What's your name?" he asked.

"Beth. But..." Her head jerked, and she looked around. "I need...Nate."

"I'll find him for you." Darlene was on duty today, but something told Blake this was more than she could handle on her own. Beth was going to need a doctor.

Before he reached the porch, another engine rumbled down the drive. When he glanced over his shoulder and spotted Shannon pulling into the yard, a sense of relief swept over him. She might not be a doctor, but as far as he was concerned, she was the next best thing.

She had to be as surprised by their unexpected visitor and her condition as he was. He'd try to offer what little explanation he had as soon as he got Beth out of the rain.

"What's going on?" Shannon asked.

Blake paused under the cover of the porch. "This is Beth. Apparently Nate is a friend of hers. She seems to think he can help her, but she's going to need medical care. And quickly."

"Take her to the office."

As Blake complied, Shannon followed a step or two behind him. "Do you have any idea what happened?"

"Apparently someone named Kenny has a bad temper. I'm not sure how Nate plays into it, but he's already gone home for the day."

Darlene, the nurse who'd been called in to work, was just coming down the hall when Blake and Shannon entered the house. "Oh, my God. What happened?"

"We're not sure," Shannon said. "But you'd better get out of here, Darlene. The creek was rising fast when I drove over the bridge. You'll be stuck here if you don't leave soon."

"I can stay if you need me," Darlene said. "Although, I did promise my sister I'd babysit for her tonight."

Shannon shook her head. "No, go on home."

Once Blake set Beth on the small exam table in the medical office, he stepped back, making room for Shannon. But he continued to study her, noting the blood that matted her hair, the bruises and cuts on her face. He wasn't a medical professional. but it was easy to see she was in bad shape and needed to be in a hospital.

"Would you call 9-1-1?" Shannon asked. "She needs an ambulance—or a Life Flight helicopter if they can't drive over the bridge."

"Yes. I'll also tell the dispatcher to alert the police."

What kind of bastard would beat a pregnant woman? And what about the baby? Had it suffered any life-threatening injuries? Blake rushed to the telephone, only to find there wasn't a dial tone. Damn. Now what?

He returned to the office and gave Shannon the news—help wasn't on the way.

"Then I'll do what I can for her. We'll just have to pray the phone works soon."

As Shannon began to examine Beth, Blake took a step back. He was reluctant to leave the room, though. For some reason, he felt a part of the unfolding drama.

"How far along is she?" he asked.

Shannon carefully probed Beth's womb. "My guess is about six or seven months. It's hard to say."

"Is the baby okay?"

"It's moving, but that's about all I can tell you. She needs an obstetrician—and an ER. We're just not set up to handle this sort of emergency."

"I'll try calling again in a few minutes," Blake said. Shannon merely nodded, her focus on her patient.

Moments later, thunder shook the house, followed by a crack of lightning. As the rain began to pound the window, Beth cried out and clutched her belly.

If Shannon was worried, she didn't show it. Instead, she moved competently around her patient, washing her face with gentle hands and whispering words of comfort. "You're going to be fine. And so is your little one."

Blake had no other choice but to take her at her word. Beth would pull through—and so would the baby. But when she screamed again, he wasn't so sure.

"Would you please try the telephone again?" Shannon asked. "I think she's in labor."

He hoped that wasn't the case, especially if she was two to three months early. But when he reached for the telephone on Shannon's desk and tried to dial out, he was again met with dead silence.

In the old days, this was the time the men were asked to boil water. He doubted that was necessary, but it might not be a bad idea to make some coffee. Something told him this was going to be a long night.

As he headed down the hall, Joy met him. "Darlene met us on the road and told us about the woman who was battered. Can I do anything to help?"

"I'm not sure. Maybe you should brew a pot of coffee." Blake paused and blew out a sigh. "And would you please try calling 9-1-1 periodically? That woman needs to be in a hospital."

Joy nodded, then hurried toward the kitchen. In the meantime, Blake returned to the office to be there for Shannon. He didn't doubt her competency for a moment, but he wanted to offer some moral support.

He also intended to protect her and her patient. He didn't want to think about what might happen if Kenny had followed Beth here. But he'd keep that scenario to himself.

"How's she doing?" he asked.

Shannon glanced at the laboring woman, who seemed to be drifting in and out of consciousness. "Hanging in there. Any luck with the telephone?"

"Not yet."

"Well, then for the time being, it looks like I'm all Beth has."

"You'll do fine," Blake said. "And if you need a teammate, just say the word. I'll do whatever you need me to do."

He just hoped they'd both be enough.

Chapter Eleven

The wind howled outside, and the tree branches scraped against the rain-splattered office window. Inside the house, it was warm and dry, but that didn't mean all was well.

After Blake stepped out of the office for a cup of coffee, Shannon donned a pair of surgical gloves and examined Beth, who was unconscious. All the while, she spoke softly, hoping to comfort the woman if she woke up, but she didn't react at all.

Just as Shannon feared, her membranes had ruptured and labor had begun. This wasn't good.

She'd do everything in her power to help the woman, of course, but her only medical supplies and equipment were those that covered minor emergencies, so her hands were somewhat tied.

Unless they could transport Beth to the hospital, the outlook wasn't good for either the mother or the baby.

Shannon tossed the gloves into the trash can just as Blake entered the office carrying two mugs of coffee. He handed one to Shannon. He'd even added cream and sweetener, just the way she liked it.

"Thanks," she said. "It's going to be a long night."

"How's she doing? Has anything changed?"

"Her water broke, she's having strong contractions and she's beginning to dilate." When Shannon spotted his concerned expression, she added, "But she isn't aware of any pain or discomfort."

"Something tells me that's not necessarily a good thing."

It wasn't. Shannon was worried about her head injuries, any one of which could mean Kenny's blows had fractured her skull. Beth needed an MRI, but she wouldn't get one here.

Joy, who stood in the office doorway with Sam, said, "I made some chicken soup in case you get hungry later. I also made up the spare bed in Rex's room. Beth might be more comfortable in there."

"Thanks," Shannon said. "I'm sure you're right."

"Sam and I can move her." Blake set his coffee mug on the desk, then motioned for his uncle's help.

Moments later, the men had gently carried Beth into the other room and placed her on top of the mattress. She stirred and moaned while they worked, but she didn't actually wake up.

Joy slipped out of the bedroom for a few minutes.

When she returned, Shannon said, "Maybe you and Sam should turn in for the night and get some rest."

"All right, we will. But please come and get us if you need us—or if we can do anything at all." Joy reached for Sam's hand. "Just so you know, I'll put it in the refrigerator. If you need it, you'll just have to warm it up."

When the older couple left, Shannon turned to Blake. "You might as well take off, too."

"I'm not going anywhere. I'm in this with you. Is there anything I can do?"

"Not that I can think of." Just his presence alone was comforting, but she hated to admit that. Besides, she'd learned early on that, as long as she stayed calm and in control, those around her would remain that way, too.

Then an idea struck. "Did Beth have a purse?"

"I didn't see one. She might have left home in a hurry and neglected to grab it. It's also possible she left it in her vehicle. I'll go outside and look."

"Thanks. Maybe it will give us a clue about who she is or who her doctor is." Of course, without a telephone or any way to contact her obstetrician, it wouldn't help much.

Moments later, Blake returned to the bedroom with a small black tote, one of the straps attached to the bag by a safety pin. "I found this on the seat, near the passenger side. I assume you want me to do some detective work."

"That's exactly what I had in mind."

Blake took a seat on the edge of Rex's bed, then began to empty Beth's bag. While he pulled out a wallet and several scraps of paper, Shannon went back to the office to try the phone again, but she still couldn't get through. So she returned to her patient's bedside.

"Did you learn anything?" she asked Blake.

"Her name is Elizabeth Brennan. She'll be twenty in November and lives in Wexler. At least, that's the address on her driver's license. I found an appointment reminder card. It looks like her obstetrician is Dr. Selena Ramirez. Apparently her next checkup is on Friday."

"At least she's had prenatal care, so that's good. And now I know who to contact when the phone works again."

"For what it's worth," Blake added, "I checked the glove box while I was getting her purse from the pickup. The vehicle is registered to Kenneth Brennan."

"The guy who beat her? 'Kenny' is her husband?"

"That's my guess."

Shannon slowly shook her head. She understood the dynamics involved in domestic abuse, but that didn't mean they didn't upset her. "I guess Beth was desperate to escape, but why was she looking for Nate?"

"There was an envelope on the seat, but it didn't have a letter in it. Nate had sent it to her, using the Rocking C for his return address."

Shannon glanced at the battered woman lying on the bed. "I wonder what was going on between them. Could she be Nate's sister?"

"We won't know anything until we can talk to Nate."

"And we can't do that until the phone is working again." Shannon's focus returned to her patient.

After Blake put everything back into Beth's purse, he pulled up a chair next to Shannon and glanced at Beth. "How's she doing now?"

"About the same, but her contractions are getting stronger." Shannon leaned back in her seat. "I feel so helpless."

Blake reached out and took her hand, giving it a warm, gentle squeeze. "You're amazing. Don't ever forget that."

She turned to him and smiled. "Thanks, I appreciate you saying that."

"I mean every word of it." Something sparked in his eyes—respect, compassion and... Could it be *love*?

Had he begun the feel the same way about her as she was feeling for him?

She didn't dare make any assumptions, but there was something to be said about having a man at her side, a teammate who was giving his all—win or lose.

And she couldn't help wondering if Blake would be that loyal and dedicated to his lover.

Or to his wife.

Throughout the night, Blake stuck close to Shannon's side, providing her with his support, as well as any help she might need. Every once in a while, he'd leave and go into the office to see if the telephone was working. He knew better than to even try his cell. The reception in the valley was crappy at best.

Finally, around two o'clock, he heard a dial tone and quickly placed the 9-1-1 call, providing the details of their emergency.

Shannon must have heard him talking to the dispatcher because she followed him to the phone and stood by to make sure that help was on the way.

Unfortunately, when Blake replaced the old-style receiver into the cradle, he didn't have good news for her. "It's going to be a while before the paramedics can get here. There was a bad accident on the interstate involving a big rig, a tour bus and several other cars. So the first responders are going to be tied up for a while."

Concern splashed across Shannon's face. "That might be too late. Beth's contractions are coming about three minutes apart, and she's about five centimeters dilated. I'm also worried about the fact that she's still unconscious. If she can't push the baby out, she's going to need a C-section."

Blake watched as tears filled her eyes. He'd never been able to deal with a woman's emotions, but this was different. Shannon was different.

As he slipped his arms around her and drew her close, she leaned into him and rested her head on his shoulder. He breathed in the soft, floral scent of her shampoo, savoring it, and closed his eyes. He wished he could offer her more than support, although he had no idea what he could possibly provide her.

"Do you have Nate's telephone number?" he asked. "Maybe we should call him now that the line is open. He might have more information about Beth and her pregnancy."

"Good idea." Shannon went to the personnel file, and after locating the number, called the ranch hand's house. As seconds ticked away, her brow furrowed. Then she hung up the receiver and turned to Blake in disbelief. "He didn't answer. I wonder where he'd be at two in the morning."

A single man on his night off? Maybe he was at a bar with a few buddies and got stuck in town when the storm hit. Or he might have been on a date that had ended in a sleepover. Blake didn't find that unusual at all.

Before he could tell Shannon as much, she stiffened. "Oh, no. You don't think Nate was involved in that accident on the interstate, do you?"

"Don't worry about that now. Let's focus on helping Beth and her little one."

She nodded, sucked in a deep breath then headed back to her patient.

As tough as this night had been, something good had come of it. Blake had seen Shannon in action, and he'd been impressed with her skill, with her compassion. No wonder she'd wanted to be a doctor. She would have made a damn good one.

But that hadn't been the only conclusion he'd come to. During the crisis, he and Shannon had become a team of sorts. And he liked the thought of that, as well as the sense of warmth and unity it had evoked.

Twenty minutes later, the whirring of a helicopter sounded outside, its blades circling as it hovered overhead. It had to be Life Flight. That assumption was confirmed when Joy and Sam, who'd apparently been awakened by the noise, escorted a flight nurse and paramedic into the bedroom, where Beth lay—still unconscious.

When Shannon had caught them up to speed and given them the obstetrician's name, they placed the pregnant woman on a gurney and rushed her out of the house.

Once they were gone, Shannon's shoulders slumped, and she let out a ragged sigh.

"Honey," Joy said, "you need to get some rest."

"I know, but..." Shannon didn't have to finish. They all knew what she was about to say. Not only was she the head nurse, but she was the only one on duty tonight and possibly all day tomorrow.

"Sam and I will watch over the men here," Joy said. "You won't do anyone any good if you don't get some sleep."

Shannon bit down on her bottom lip. "I suppose you're right."

Blake reached out, took her hand in his and gave it a warm squeeze. "Come with me to Sam's place. It's quiet there, and you can take a good nap."

"That's a great idea," Joy said. "I'll call you there if we need you, and you can come back."

As Shannon pondered the suggestion, Blake added, "I'll stay awake and listen for the phone. You won't be neglecting your duty. You'll still be on the premises and only minutes away from the residents."

"Okay," she said. "Give me a minute to grab my toothbrush, a change of clothes and a few other things."

As Blake watched her walk away, he couldn't help

but smile at the irony. He'd wanted to get Shannon in his bed before he left for California, but this wasn't quite what he'd had in mind.

The rain had stopped shortly before Shannon and Blake dashed outside and made a run to Sam's place, their feet sloshing on the wet grass. After leaving their shoes on the small front porch, they entered the cozy living room.

So far, Blake had been a perfect host, as well as a gentleman. He'd told her to make herself at home, then he showed her the bathroom, making sure she had a washcloth and a couple of fresh towels.

Then he'd left her alone so she could get ready for bed. After she washed her face and brushed her teeth, she slipped on her nightclothes, a pair of gray flannel boxers and an oversized white shirt. For a moment she wished she'd grabbed something a little newer, a little sexier, but she quickly scolded herself for having that stray thought.

She was here to take a nap—nothing else. Besides, she was so exhausted, so emotionally spent, that she would probably fall asleep the moment her head hit the pillow.

Still, when she stepped out of the bathroom and found Blake standing barefoot near the double bed, the covers turned down for her, she tugged at the hem of her shirt.

"Do you need anything?" he asked.

Oh, she had needs all right. But she couldn't very well discuss them with him. "I'm fine. Just…a little tired."

Still, she continued to study him as he stood there, his hair damp from the rain.

Would he walk away now and leave her to sleep? Or would he say something more to her, prolonging their time together? Maybe he'd even offer her a goodnight kiss.

Either way, she wasn't quite ready for him to leave. If she gave him an appreciative hug and a kiss, would it be out of line?

She didn't think so. He'd been a real trouper this evening, even though he'd had every reason to leave her to deal with Beth on her own. It's not like he had any medical training or experience. But he'd obviously sensed that she'd needed his emotional support. And the fact that he'd acted on that not only pleased her, but touched her heart.

"Thanks for hanging out with me tonight." She crossed the room, joining him near the bed. "I usually handle emergency situations by rote. My training just kicks in. But I wasn't prepared for a case like Beth's."

"I know, but you did everything you possibly could for her."

"I'm just glad she's finally at the hospital, where someone can properly care for her."

As if sensing what she wanted to do and why she was hesitant to make the first move, he opened his arms for her. Without missing a beat, she stepped into his embrace as if it was the most natural thing in the world for her to do.

And who was to say that it wasn't?

Blake felt so good, so right. And while she knew

that he'd only meant to offer her comfort and understanding in a time of crisis, she wanted more from him. She needed more.

Without pondering the repercussions, she slipped her hands around his neck, then drew his lips to hers.

Blake had been thinking about kissing Shannon all evening long, but the moment had never been right. Even minutes ago, when she'd been in the bathroom, he'd contemplated his desire, pondered his options and considered the limits he might want to set.

Now, as their bodies pressed together, their hands stroked each other, caressing and exploring. Before he knew it, his common sense deserted him, and his libido took its place. He couldn't seem to get enough of Shannon's taste, of her soft, warm body.

When his hand reached her breast, covered only by a thin piece of cotton, he fondled it. As his thumb skimmed a taut nipple, her breath caught. He damn near gasped, too.

He'd never wanted a woman this badly, never felt as though he needed her, that he might find something special in her arms that no one else could provide.

He pulled his lips from hers long enough to trail kisses along the side of her neck and down to her throat. But he wasn't content to leave it at that. He reached for the hem of her shirt and lifted it up, revealing her breasts and the dusky nipples he wanted to take in his mouth, to tongue until her breath caught again.

After she helped with the removal of her night

shirt, he ravished one breast, then the other until a surge of heat and desire shot through him. He straightened and kissed her again, deeply, thoroughly. Then he pulled her hips flush against his erection, taunting them both to the breaking point.

He reached for the waistband of her boxer shorts and slipped them over her hips. She helped him shove them all the way down, stepped out of them and kicked them aside.

Her naked body, petite and lithe, was everything he'd imagined it to be and more. And, at least for tonight, she was his.

"I want you to take your clothes off, too," she said. "I need to feel your skin against mine."

"There's nothing I'd like more than to make love with you."

When he'd shed his shirt and removed his jeans and briefs, she studied his body as intently as he'd studied hers.

Taking mercy on them both, he lifted her in his arms and placed her on top of the mattress. Her dark hair splayed upon the white pillow, her body upon the light blue bedspread.

Before he could take a moment to fully appreciate her beauty, she reached for him, pulling him down with her.

He continued to kiss her, to taste her, to stroke her until they were both ready to scream. Then, as if gathering her senses, she drew back. "I sure hope you have a condom."

"I always keep one in my shaving kit."

She let out a little sigh of relief, and he laughed. "Hold that thought. I'll be right back."

When he returned and had protected them both, he again joined her in bed. And they took up again right where they'd left off. As he hovered over her, she reached for his sheathed erection and guided him right where he wanted to be. Where he needed to be.

He'd meant to enter her slowly, but he was so eager to join his body with hers, that he thrust deep inside. Again her breath caught, but she arched up to meet him, matching each of his in and out movements with her own. As she reached a peak, she cried out with her release. He couldn't have prolonged his own any longer, even if he'd wanted to. And they came together in a mind-swirling, earth-shaking climax.

Making love with Shannon had been unimaginable, and far better than he'd ever thought sex could be.

There seemed to be much more going on between them than physical attraction, chemistry and lust. In fact, lying in Shannon's arms, he felt as though he'd finally...come home.

As the sun peered through the cracks in the bedroom blinds, Shannon stretched out her arm onto the other side of the mattress, where Blake had lain earlier while they'd enjoyed the sweet afterglow. He'd promised to stay awake in case Joy called, so he'd eventually rolled out of bed and let Shannon sleep.

Since the phone hadn't rung and he hadn't knocked, she suspected that all was going well at the big house. But here at Sam's place? Things had gone better than well.

Last night, Blake had shown her the tender loving care she'd so often dealt out but rarely received. And she loved him for it.

Correction. She just plain loved *him*.

She glanced at the clock on the nightstand. 6:33 a.m. It was time to dispense the morning medication, and Blake needed to get some sleep, too. So she threw off the covers and got out of bed. Then she padded to the bathroom, took a shower and ran a brush through her hair, sweeping her curls into a messy topknot.

After dressing, she went to look for Blake and found him in the small living area, stretched out on the sofa, watching a golf match on television with the volume turned off.

When he looked up and spotted her, a grin stole across his face. "Good morning. I was just about to come in there and wake you. How'd you sleep?"

"Better than I expected. Are you going to be able to catch a little shut-eye now?"

"Probably. Then I'm going to drive out and check the water level of the creek myself. I need to go to the airport as soon as I can get there."

Her heart twisted. He was still talking about rushing home? Even after last night?

Of course he was. She couldn't expect him not to. But wasn't he going to at least mention what they'd done, what they'd shared?

Wasn't there any kind of future for them—together?

They'd needed to have that kind of conversation after their first heated kiss, but they hadn't. And now that they'd actually made love, that discussion was all the more important.

"You know," he said, "I've been thinking."

Oh, good. That was a relief. She would have hated to be the one to broach the subject herself.

"Thinking about what?" she prompted.

"For one thing, we have a good thing going. And I'd hate to lose that."

Hope soared, filling her chest to the brim. "And for another?"

"I was thinking about you attending medical school."

She tilted her head, trying to wrap her mind around his comment. "I'm not following you."

"You'd make a good doctor, and I think you should chase your dream. In fact, I'll pay the tuition, if you choose a school in Southern California. That way, we can have a relationship and I can go back to work at my firm. The way I see it, everyone wins."

"Excuse me?"

"Think about it," he said. "Your skills and bedside manner are better suited to being a doctor. And if you choose a school near me, it won't cost you anything."

She was stunned. What in the heck was going on? He wasn't suggesting a "relationship," he was making a business deal. What he was offering was no better than a bribe. What was he thinking? That she was only interested in what he had to offer her—or that she could be...bought?

And what *bedside* manner was he talking about?

The one she'd displayed just for him in this very house?

"I'm not interested in leaving Texas." Not if it meant being his paid mistress or whatever he had in mind.

How had she let this happen? She'd seen his flaws and shortcomings, but time and again she'd overlooked them.

But she never should have overlooked the money issue. Blake put way too much value on having it, keeping it and using it to his best advantage.

She slowly shook her head. When he first arrived at the ranch, he'd thought Joy was after Sam's money. And now he'd made the same assumption about her. But Shannon didn't give a darn about anything he might or might not have stockpiled in banks. She wasn't swayed by his wealth. Neither she nor her affections were for sale.

"What's the matter?" he asked, as she reached for the doorknob. "Are you upset about something?"

"I'm just…" When she glanced over her shoulder to give him a final look, her heart twisted again, this time into a wadded-up mess. Her eyes misted, but she managed to keep her voice steady. "Apparently you have the wrong impression of me, and I doubt there's anything I can do to change that."

Needing to get away before she burst into tears, she opened the door and closed it soundly behind her.

Chapter Twelve

The rain had finally moved on, but Blake kept to himself for the next twenty-four hours by eating whatever he could find in Sam's pantry. Hopefully he wouldn't have to live off canned chili beans or peanut butter sandwiches much longer.

He expected the road to open up again soon, if it hadn't already. Then he could finally leave the ranch and put Shannon behind him.

He wasn't happy about whatever had gone wrong between them, especially after the amazing night they'd spent in bed. But he still had no real explanation for it.

After she'd left him yesterday morning, practically slamming the door behind her, he'd gone over and over the last conversation they'd had. She'd been upset by something, but he wasn't exactly sure what.

He suspected it had been the stipulations he'd put on his offer to pay for her medical school tuition that had set her off. She might not have liked the parameters limiting her choices. Obviously she'd planned to attend a school in Texas. But didn't she realize that he'd only meant to provide a way for them to live closer to each other, to...be together? He hadn't meant to use his offer as a dangling carrot. Had she thought that's what he'd tried to do?

It's just that he'd been so caught up in admiration for her, not to mention the great chemistry they had, that he'd begun to feel...

Well, he wasn't ready to go so far as to say that it might be love, but whatever it was had compelled him to offer her the world, at least his little corner of it.

That wasn't something to be taken lightly. But she had, and it hurt like hell.

He ought to cut bait and run, just as he had from Melissa when he'd realized she was only involved with him because of the life he could provide her, the things he could buy. In fact, he'd been so angry with himself and so disgusted by the woman Melissa had turned out to be, that breaking up with her and shutting her out of his life had been fairly easy.

So why couldn't he get Shannon out of his mind?

Because, in spite of the skepticism he'd once had, Shannon wasn't anything like Melissa. And walking away from her, from what they might have had together would be a lot more complicated—and far more painful.

He had to do something to make things right, although he wasn't sure what.

Should he approach her with a peace offering? No, that wouldn't work. This wasn't something he could buy his way out of.

Did she realize that it wasn't just about the cost of the schooling he'd offered her? He'd actually thought they had something special. That he might even...

He slowly shook his head and reeled in his thoughts. It was hard enough to express all he'd felt—all he was still feeling—for her, even in his own mind.

Could it be love? It certainly was strong enough to be, although the idea alone was foreign to him and difficult to understand, let alone admit.

He'd once thought that *real* love, the unconditional, I-need-you-to-be-at-my-side-forever kind that Sam and Nellie once had, would always escape him.

It certainly would if he didn't do something about Shannon. But what? Something told him that this time an apology alone wasn't going to cut it.

Could he actually do something far more difficult and frightening than that? Could he open up his heart and tell Shannon what he might be feeling for her?

But what if she threw his heart right back in his face?

After finishing off the last of the coffee he'd made early that morning, he ate the peach cobbler Joy had brought over to him last night. He considered it breakfast, although he would've preferred something heartier, healthier.

He washed the dishes and put them away, then headed for the door. He planned to drive out to the bridge and check the level of the creek to see if it had gone down. Hoping for the best, he'd already packed his bag and had it in the truck. He had to get out of here in the worst way. And before the emotional quagmire he'd found himself in revealed his vulnerability. Only trouble was, he feared it would follow him all the way home, along with Shannon's memory.

As his thoughts and feelings continued to tumble around in his brain, he headed outside. He'd no more than stepped into the warm sunshine when he spotted his uncle striding across the yard.

Blake would tell Sam he was leaving, but that he'd be back. He just wasn't entirely sure when that would be.

When Sam spotted Blake's approach, he stopped in his tracks and placed his hands on his hips. "Did you finally decide to come out of your cave?"

"I had a lot of thinking to do."

Sam merely nodded, as if he understood the questions that had been bombarding him since Shannon had walked out on him.

"You get it figured out?" he finally asked.

No, but maybe he would. Eventually. "I'm going to drive out to the bridge and see if I can get through."

"Don't bother. The road's open. Nate made it through this morning."

"Did you tell him about Beth?"

"Yep. Sure did. He jumped right back in his truck and hightailed it to the hospital."

Last night, when Joy had brought him that dessert, she'd told him that Beth's baby girl had been delivered by Caesarean. The three-pound preemie was doing okay, although she'd be in the neonatal intensive care unit for a month or more. Beth, on the other hand, still hadn't come to.

But maybe things had changed.

"How's Beth doing this morning?" Blake asked.

"She's in a coma. Doc Nelson said they don't expect her to pull through. That jerk she married beat her to a pulp, causing a brain bleed, among other things."

"Did Nate say why Beth had been looking for him?"

"Apparently she'd split from her husband about a year ago. She and Nate dated for a while. But then she got a wild hair and went back to the abuser."

"Does Nate think she came looking for him hoping to have a second chance?"

"I'm not sure what she was thinking, other than to escape that brute, but she'd told Nate a couple of months back that she was pregnant and that the baby was his. Nate wrote to her, telling her where she could find him if she ever needed him."

"I guess, after that beating, she decided she needed all the help she could get if she wanted to get away once and for all."

"That's my guess. Nate thinks the guy figured out the baby wasn't his and flipped out."

Blake couldn't imagine what he'd do if he ever found himself the father of a premature newborn.

"So what's eating *you*?" Sam asked.

Blake wasn't eager to share his confusion, but Sam usually had good advice. And more than once, Blake really should have followed it.

"I told Shannon I'd pay for her medical school if

she found one in California. And for some reason it set her off."

"Why'd you offer to do something like that?"

"Because I wanted her to know how I felt about her. And I wanted to tempt her to move to California."

Sam swore under his breath. "For a man who's supposed to be so dadgum bright, you sure don't have a lick of sense when it comes to life or to women."

Blake wanted to object, but right now, it seemed as though the older man had a point.

"You said you wanted to *show* her," Sam said. "And sometimes a man has to do that. But did you ever *tell* her how you were feeling?"

"Not exactly. I… Well, it's hard to put into words."

"Do you love her?"

That had to be it since he'd never felt anything like it before. But even admitting it to Sam wasn't easy.

"I've always kept my feelings close to the vest," Blake said.

"You sound like your granddad. And how did that work for him? He and his wife never did seem very affectionate toward each other, and the last time I saw her, she looked miserable."

"Maybe I owe Shannon an apology."

Sam humphed. "For what? Attempting to bribe her or buy her affections?"

"That's not what I did. At least, I didn't do it intentionally."

Sam clucked his tongue. "No wonder that redhead tried to take you to the cleaners."

"Melissa? What're you getting at?"

"When you use money to try and please—or lure—women, you tend to attract the ones who can be bought. You probably also give off the vibe that you don't believe in love and don't want to get married, so women with a real heart, women like Shannon, leave you in the dust."

It all began to fall into place, finally making sense. Damn. No wonder Shannon had been so upset. He'd been an ass, even though he hadn't meant to be.

"You've spent years cheating yourself out of having an emotional bond with someone you really care about," Sam said. "And you show off your Achilles' heel to the very folks who shouldn't be seeing it."

Blake had never wanted anyone to spot any vulnerability in him, which was why he kept his feelings to himself.

"If you're flaunting your money rather than your feelings, how can you blame a greedy person for thinking you'd be a good catch?"

Melissa had certainly had a greedy streak. But had Blake given her reason to believe he'd pave the road to her future with gold and diamonds?

"Shannon isn't the least bit selfish," Sam said. "She's got a warm and loving heart, and when it comes to finding a perfect mate and a loyal partner for life, she's the real McCoy."

Sam was right. And Blake had been a fool.

"Shannon isn't the kind of woman who'd want you to pay for her schooling. If she loves you, too, all she wants is your heart."

Maybe so, but there lay the problem. Blake had

protected his heart for so long, it was the one thing he was reluctant to reveal, let alone give away.

But did Shannon love him, too?

He'd never know unless he told her how he was feeling "I'd better go look for her."

"She's not on the ranch. She left early this morning."

Blake's gut clenched. "Where'd she go?"

"I'm not sure. She called Alicia and asked her to cover for her until Chloe could find someone to re-place her as the head nurse. But I think she was going to stop at the hospital first. She wanted to check on her patients."

A dedicated nurse would do that. And so would a woman with a loving heart.

Blake wasn't sure what he'd say to her when he found her, but he knew that this time an apology and a bouquet of roses wouldn't be enough.

Once Shannon arrived at the medical center, she stopped to check on Beth in the ICU. She wasn't a family member, so she didn't expect anyone to tell her anything specific about the young woman's med-ical condition. But she'd hoped to learn something.

Fortunately, she ran into Doc Nelson in the hall. He told her what she'd heard last night, that Beth wasn't expected to recover.

"Does she show any sign of brain activity?" she asked Doc.

"No, although they're still running tests." He placed a hand on Shannon's shoulder and gave it a gentle squeeze. "It's never easy to lose a patient. But it might give you a bit of satisfaction to know that

Beth's husband was arrested and charged with assault last night. And if she dies, that charge will change to murder."

"I sure hope she pulls out of it," Shannon said, not only thinking about the young woman, but also her baby.

"Sadly, that's doubtful."

Shannon had been afraid he'd say that, but she thanked him for the update and let him get back to his patients.

Her next stop was the NICU. She wouldn't be allowed to enter, but she wanted to get a glimpse of the baby.

When she peered into the window and scanned the incubators, she spotted Nate standing near one that held a preemie, which had to be Beth's daughter. When he glanced up and saw Shannon at the window, he moved to the door, removed the hospital gown he'd been wearing over his clothes and the disposable booties over his shoes. Then he joined her in the corridor.

"How's the baby doing?" she asked.

"Holding her own, but they say Beth probably won't make it." He raked a hand through his short hair.

"I'm sorry." Shannon's words were sincere, yet they seemed so inadequate.

Nate blew out a sigh, then looked down at his scuffed boots. When he glanced up, he said, "She told me I was the baby's father. And I could be, but I'm not totally convinced."

"You can always ask for a paternity test."

He raked a hand through his hair. "I won't do

that. I'm afraid the results might prove she's Kenny's daughter, and I'd rather die than see him get custody of that sweet little girl."

Shannon was sure Beth would agree—if she could.

"I still have the letter she wrote," Nate said. "The one that claims the baby is mine."

Yes, but Kenny was Beth's husband. And while Shannon wasn't sure about the legalities, she suspected that letter might not be enough. Nate would need to talk to a lawyer, but the poor man didn't need anything else to worry about now.

After telling Nate goodbye, Shannon headed for the elevator so she could visit Rex. When she reached the third floor and entered his room, she found him sleeping. She could have left and come back later, but she had nowhere better to go. In fact, just being here, in a hospital setting, helped set her back on...

Well, she wasn't on an even keel just yet. Her heart still ached after being reminded of what she'd known all along: Blake Darnell was a career-driven, manipulative man who didn't have a loving bone in his body.

As if sensing her presence in the doorway, Rex cracked open one eye, then the other. When he spotted Shannon, he broke into a grin. "Boy, am I glad to see you. I was afraid I was going to wake up hearing harp music, fluttering wings and angel voices." He chuckled. "But that would be a lot better than seeing crackling flames or feeling heat."

She smiled as she made her way to his bedside. "Don't worry, Rex. You're still among the living."

"I would have figured that out soon enough. My

prostate keeps reminding me that I'm still alive and kicking. Dang it. I have to pee like a son of a gun." He threw off the covers, rolled to the side of the bed and used the bedrail to help himself up.

"Want some help?" she asked, willing to assist but expecting him to tell her not to bother.

"Nope. I can do it." He let his bare feet dangle near the floor. "Just give me a minute so the ol' ticker has time to get the blood flowing in the right direction."

He stepped onto the floor and winced.

"Are you okay?" she asked.

"Just that blasted knee. About five years back, Doc Nelson said it was rubbing bone on bone. If I'd known I was going to live this long, I might have let him talk me into having the darn thing replaced."

"It's not too late to have that surgery," she said.

"The hell it isn't. Besides, why let them cut me up now? I'm not going to run any more foot races." He chuckled. "'Course I do need to trot to the john every now and then."

Rex had no more than made his way into the bathroom when a knock sounded on the doorjamb.

Shannon turned, expecting to see a nurse, an aide or even Doc Nelson. Instead she spotted Blake. Her heart clenched, and her stomach twisted into a knot.

What in the world was he doing here?

Blake had feared that Shannon might have left the hospital before he arrived, but he was in luck.

The only problem was, by the scrunched brow that marred her pretty face, he could tell she clearly wasn't happy to see him.

Instead of her typical workday attire of hospital scrubs, she had on a pair of jeans, as well as a light green blouse. Too bad she wasn't also wearing a smile.

"I assume you came to visit Rex," she said. "He's in the bathroom."

"Actually, it's you I came to see. I need to talk to you."

"I'm afraid I was just leaving." She reached for her purse, which was sitting on the edge of the bed, slipped her arm through the strap and let it hang from her shoulder.

"Don't go yet," he said.

She folded her arms across her chest, her body language telling him she'd shut him off before he'd uttered a single word. "What do you want to talk about?"

"For one thing, I need to apologize."

She arched a delicate brow. "Without any chocolate or roses?"

"Would they have helped?"

Her only answer was to shake her head.

"I'm sorry if I offended you."

Before he could continue his speech, she interrupted. "Offended me? You dangled my dream in front of me, just like a carrot, hoping to control me so I'd go along with anything you wanted me to do. But it didn't work. I never should have gotten involved with you in the first place. What's more, I'm not going to California—for school or any other reason."

Nope. The flowers and chocolate wouldn't have even come close to helping him repair the mess he'd made this time.

She didn't appear to be especially mad, though.

Actually, he was much better at handling anger. Instead, she was hurt—and deeply. That was going to be a whole lot more difficult because the touchy-feely stuff always threw him off stride.

But he was ready to go to any length to get back on her good side. "I didn't mean to attach conditions to that offer. I only did it because I wanted you to live closer to me—or even with me. I feel something for you, Shannon. Something I've never felt for anyone before."

"Then why did you try to bribe me? Why couldn't you just come out and talk to me? Were you afraid to admit what you were feeling, whatever that might have been?"

She'd hit the nail square on the head. His knee-jerk reaction was to deny the truth. Instead, he needed to explain. "For most of my adult life and a lot of my childhood, I wasn't encouraged to feel anything at all—anger, grief, frustration. Or even love. Keeping things locked up inside became a habit."

"A bad one." She slowly shook her head. "What's worse, I've been looking for a man like my father, a man who is strong enough to tell me he loves me, to show me in a million different ways—but never with money or gifts."

"I can try to be that man."

As tears filled her eyes, he felt compelled to cross the room and take her in his arms, to press her head against his shoulder, to tell her he loved her from here to eternity. But in spite of his resolve to be more open with her, he suspected his claims and promises wouldn't be enough.

Even though he feared hearing her answer, he asked, "What's the matter? Why are you crying?"

"Because you'll never be that man I was looking for, but it's too late anyway. My plan to find him was ruined when I met you. I didn't mean to, but I fell in love with you—not my dream guy."

Blake's heart soared.

She must have sensed his excitement because she added, "But I'm working on falling out of love, just as quickly as I fell in."

Blake doubted that would happen so quickly, and he took it as a positive sign. Before he could cross the room and sweep Shannon into his arms, the bathroom door creaked open, and Rex came out wearing a crooked grin.

"Don't pay me any mind," he said, as he limped toward his bed. "I've enjoyed hearing the show so far, but I'll be more comfortable if I stretch out and watch the action."

Blake couldn't help but chuckle. That old cowboy might come across as grouchy at times, but he was a real kick. He could easily become a friend. Either way, Blake was determined to move heaven and earth to make sure Rex remained at the Rocking Chair Ranch for the rest of his life.

Shannon approached the bed and watched Rex climb in, her hands raised as though she was ready to help him if his movements faltered. When he made it on his own, she turned back to Blake. "Maybe we'd better finish this discussion somewhere else."

He didn't care where they talked, as long as they got things said—and settled between them. But it was high time he admitted his feelings for her, no matter who was listening.

"Actually, it's probably best if I have a witness. I love you, Shannon. And just for the record, I'd be happy to pay your tuition to attend the medical school of your choice—no strings attached. Just follow your heart, honey. If you want to stay in Texas, I'll move here, too, so we can be together. That is, if you'll have me."

She gaped at him. "Are you *kidding*?"

"I've never been more serious. Now that I've met you, I won't be happy living anywhere unless you're with me, or at least, nearby."

"You'd leave California?" she asked. "What about your law practice?"

"I've passed the bar in Texas, too. So I can hang up my shingle here." Blake glanced at Rex and grinned. "Besides, I already have my first client."

"Actually," Shannon said, "you're going to have a second one soon. Nate might need your services, too."

"See? There." Blake's heart began to soar. "Things are falling into place already."

When she didn't object, the emotion he'd bottled up inside for so long continued to flow out of him, the words getting easier to admit. "I'll say it again, Shannon. I love you. And I want to marry you—today, next month or whenever you set the date."

At that, Rex let out a hoot and clapped his hands. "This is one jim-dandy show. What do you say, Shannon? Don't keep the poor man hanging."

She laughed until tears spilled onto her cheeks. "I love you, too, Blake."

Then she wrapped her arms around his neck and showed him just how much.

Damn, this felt good—and not just the kiss. But Shannon, her embrace, her happiness, her love.

He couldn't wait to stand before a preacher and promise his heart to her forever, until death parted them—or maybe even longer than that.

* * * * *

Will the loner cowboy become a new daddy?
Don't miss Nate Gallagher's story in
the next installment of
ROCKING CHAIR RODEO,
the new series by
USA TODAY *Bestselling Author Judy Duarte.*
Coming soon to Mills & Boon Cherish!

MILLS & BOON®

Cherish™

EXPERIENCE THE ULTIMATE RUSH OF FALLING IN LOVE

A sneak peek at next month's titles...

In stores from 20th October 2016:

- **Christmas Baby for the Princess** – Barbara Wallace *and*
  The Maverick's Holiday Surprise – Karen Rose Smith
- **Greek Tycoon's Mistletoe Proposal** – Kandy Shepherd
  and **A Child Under His Tree** – Allison Leigh

In stores from 3rd November 2016:

- **The Billionaire's Prize** – Rebecca Winters *and*
  The Rancher's Expectant Christmas – Karen Templeton
- **The Earl's Snow-Kissed Proposal** – Nina Milne *and*
  Callie's Christmas Wish – Merline Lovelace

Just can't wait?
Buy our books online a month before they hit the shops!
www.millsandboon.co.uk

Also available as eBooks.

MILLS & BOON®

EXCLUSIVE EXCERPT

When Dea Caracciolo agrees to attend a sporting event as tycoon Guido Rossano's date, sparks fly!

Read on for a sneak preview of
THE BILLIONAIRE'S PRIZE
*the final instalment of Rebecca Winters'
thrilling Cherish trilogy*
THE MONTINARI MARRIAGES

The dark blue short-sleeved dress with small red poppies Dea was wearing hugged her figure, then flared from the waist to the knee. With every step the material danced around her beautiful legs, imitating the flounce of her hair she wore down the way he liked it. Talk about his heart failing him!

"Dea—"

Her searching gaze fused with his. "I hope it's all right." The slight tremor in her voice betrayed her fear that she wasn't welcome. If she only knew...

"You've had an open invitation since we met." Nodding his thanks to Mario, he put his arm around her shoulders and drew her inside the suite.

He slid his hands in her hair. "You're the most beautiful sight this man has ever seen." With uncontrolled hunger he lowered his mouth to hers and began to devour her. Over the announcer's voice and the roar of the crowd, he heard her little moans of pleasure as their bodies merged and they drank deeply.

When she swayed in his arms, he half carried her over to the couch where they could give in to their frenzied needs. She smelled heavenly. One kiss grew into another until she became his entire world. He'd never known a feeling like this and lost track of time and place.

"Do you know what you do to me?" he whispered against her lips with feverish intensity.

"I came for the same reason."

Her admission pulled him all the way under. Once in a while the roar of the crowd filled the room, but that didn't stop him from twining his legs with hers. He desired a closeness they couldn't achieve as long as their clothes separated them.

"I want you, *bellissima*. I want you all night long. Do you understand what I'm saying?"

Don't miss
THE BILLIONAIRE'S PRIZE
by Rebecca Winters

Available November 2016

www.millsandboon.co.uk